Alfie In a Bubble

by A.P. Walker

Order this book online at www.trafford.com
or email orders@trafford.com

Most Trafford titles are also available at major online book retailers.

Printed in Victoria, BC, Canada.

ISBN: 978-1-4269-2783-6 (sc)

Library of Congress Copyright Registration Information:
TXU000252557
1986-09-05
Copyright catalog 1978 to present.

*Our mission is to efficiently provide the world's finest, most comprehensive
book publishing service, enabling every author to experience success.
To find out how to publish your book, your way, and have it available
worldwide, visit us online at www.trafford.com*

Trafford rev. 09/16/2010

 www.trafford.com

North America & international
toll-free: 1 888 232 4444 (USA & Canada)
phone: 250 383 6864 ♦ fax: 812 355 4082

To my Sister who knew I could. To my children who said I could. To my grandchildren who are as precious to me as the sea. To my nieces and Nephews.
I love all of you.

Each wave reaches the very soul of me.
That beautiful sea,
The evenings angry sea breeze whipping hard against my face, my hair, the very soul of me;
Easing all my anxieties
And leaving me with total peace within,
Peace toward my fellow man.
How reckless and carefree you are my beautiful sea.
And as I sit beside you, that same feeling you try and give to me.
And as I look out at your waves the harder they get with fire and foam.
Beating against the rocks.
Feeling the mist of the sea against the very soul of me.
With tears and arms stretched out to you I fall and find myself ingulfed, you are surrounding me,
and all I feel is peace,
and I am worry-free..
With love, serenity,
You , my beautiful sea and me.

Contents

chapter one

FAMILY

JORDAN LEE WALKER, DEVOTED husband and father, could smile as he locked the doors of his pawnshop, the day's receipts under his arm. He provided well for his wife, Cathleen, and his two daughters, Alfie Nikol, five, and Gussie Alexis, ten. He had promised his wife Cathleen that she and the girls would never want for anything. Thoughts of his shabby childhood made that promise easy to keep. If there was a flaw in Jordan's life, it was his obsession for wealth, and being a pawnshop broker gave him the opportunity to meet with the shady criminal element who introduced Jordan to the easy money. And because Jordan owned his own Cessna 328 he was soon making weekend trips to one of the many islands in the south of Florida. He took Cathleen along to make it appear they were American tourists enjoying a holiday. But unknown to Cathleen and the authorities, a large quantity of narcotics would be stashed in Jordan's plane while he and Cathleen enjoyed the pleasures of the island.

When they returned to Miami and Jordan's plane was safely in the hangar, the narcotics were removed. Jordan never saw or touched the contraband. Yet, after each trip a substantial amount of money would be delivered in a brown manila envelope to Jordan's pawn shop. The man that delivered the money would make sure the pawn shop was empty before entering. He would lay the manila envelope on the counter, tip his hat at Jordan and then leave. No words were ever exchanged between the two men. That money along with all the honest accumulations acquired by Jordan provided his family with a wealth few people in life ever acquire. But the means that supplemented his honest income soon denied his daughters the love and security of their parents. For it was on one of these flights to the designated island that Jordan's plane developed engine failure. The plane plunged into the ocean. The bodies of Jordan and Cathleen were never retrieved from the depths of the ocean floor and buried with them was the secret that Alfie and Gussie's father had ever indulged in anything but an honest living.

Frank Varnell hailed a taxi outside the airport. He gave the cab driver the address, Miami was as humid as ever.He took out a handkerchief and wiped his forehead. The taxi's air conditioner allowed him to get his mind off of the heat. His every thought was of the two girls. He wondered if Alfie would remember him. He knew Gussie would because she was the oldest. Also, he wondered, how would the girls accept him as their guardian. The tragedy was overwhelming, and the concern for the future happiness of the two girls brought sadness to his heart. He did know that for his part, he would do everything in his power to make those girls happy. Cathleen had been all the family that he had. The bond between them had been strong. Her children were as important to him as his sister had been. And they would be the children he had never had. The cab stopped in front of the ranch-style house. One thing for sure, Frank thought, Jordon had certainly lived well. He walked up to the door and rang the bell. Yaya hugged Frank and dabbed at her eyes with the tail of her apron. She had been the housekeeper and children's nanny for six years. She was like a member of the family. Frank tried to convince Yaya to come and live with them. But he knew part of her family was in Miami and Yaya felt an even stronger tie to them since this sudden tradgey. Alfie and Gussie were quiet but their love and need for Frank was very visible. They clung to their Uncle as if he too might disappear. It would take time and a lot of love to heal the pain these small frightened girls felt. Frank had both.

chapter two

PINK SHELL ISLAND

THEY FLEW FROM THE east coast and the Atlantic to the west coast and the Pacific. And once there took a small boat to their new home. As the boat pulled up to the dock, Alfie's eyes took in the beauty of Pink Shell Island and felt a deep love that she couldn't explain. Though still grieving from the loss of her parents, she knew then that she belonged here. Frank's wife Kathy loved the girls as much as Frank did. The girls once again were part of a family. Time slowly erased the pain, and the girls blossomed like roses.

Alfie developed a bond with the sea that few people ever have. Perhaps, because the sea had become the final resting place for her parents, she felt as if it were part of her. She also loved Pink Shell Island. She enjoyed solitary walks along the shore and sitting on the rocks admiring the vastness of the sea. The sea was her friend and she talked to the "Old Man in the

Sea". The rolling waves and unmastered sound of the ocean provided a serenity that allowed her dreams of fantasy to reach the very depths of her soul. Gussie was very active and had many friends; she was just the opposite of Alfie. She grew into a tall, beautiful girl with long blond hair and big blue eyes. Uncle Frank threatened to stand guard over her to beat the boys away. Gussie would laugh as she hugged her uncle. "You're the only man I love," she told him. It was Aunt Kathy that understood Gussie and her longing to one day live in a big city. Gussie loved the Island, but to her it was confining. She wanted excitement and she would not find that here. Not the kind of excitement she read about in her True Romance magazines. Alfie was growing too. Her strawberry blond hair and extra large green eyes made her stand out from the other children on the Island. She would one day be a rare beauty.

Gussie watched as her uncle shook his head. "I'm against you working. What about your grades in school?" "Oh, Uncle Frank. You know we don't go to school in the summer. You're just trying to find a reason to keep me in the house all summer. I'm sixteen. I'm not a baby any longer. Stop treating me like one. Everyone in my class has a summer job." "Yes, I guess you are growing up. And much too pretty to stay in a house all summer." Uncle Frank walked over to Gussie and gathered her in his arms.

"The Clam Digger is a nice place. I've known Carl and Bunnie for years. They're good people. I'm just a selfish old man. I don't want you to grow up so fast." Gussie kissed his cheek. "You're the best uncle in the whole world. I love you." Alfie smiled, she knew her sister's ways. And she knew her uncle had never denied them anything. She doubted if he ever would. Frank noticed Alfie standing at the kitchen door. "Hi, Pumpkin. How about a walk on the pier?" Uncle Frank always took a walk on the pier when he was upset. So the decision of letting Gussie work had not been one he had liked. Alfie said, "Sure." She opened the hall closet and pulled her sweater from the hanger. Uncle Frank and Alfie had a special closeness. Their love for the sea was a bond between them. Alfie's love may have been a little stronger. Gussie always told her it wasn't normal to feel that way about the ocean. But Uncle Frank said it was okay, and Alfie knew it was her thoughts that mattered.

The ocean was rough and the waves were angry. Uncle Frank shook his head once again. "I sure hope it calms down. The lobster crates we put down in the harbor should be full and I want them to stay that way. Would you like to go out with me tomorrow?" Frank smiled as Alfie grabbed him around the waist and hugged hard. Alfie didn't care that it wasn't deep sea fishing that would come later when she was older. "What a question," she said. Fishing was her uncle's business and he owned four of the biggest and finest fishing boats on the Island. His only competitor was Will Kane. Alfie could hardly wait for tomorrow. Besides her uncle, she would be with Old Sarge and she loved talking to Old Sarge. He was one of the men on her uncle's boat. He told stories of the sea which were so unbelievable that they had to be true. It was through Sarge she first learned of the "Old Man in the Sea."

Her uncle, always sensitive to her moods and thoughts, asked "What are you thinking about, Alfie? The old pelican on the wharf, Old Sarge, or the `Old Man in the Sea'?" He smiled as he ruffled her hair with his hand. "The `Old Man in the Sea' is real, isn't he, uncle?" Alfie knew her uncle would say yes. And it made her feel good inside. Without waiting for her uncle to answer, Alfie continued. "I know the `Old Man in the Sea' is real. When I sit and talk to him, I can feel him answer me. Not out loud, but inside of me. Sarge said not to tell anyone that I talked to the `Old Man in the Sea' because they would laugh at me. But you talk to him, don't you, uncle?" Frank cupped his hand over the pipe to keep the match from going out in the cool ocean breeze. He puffed hard, until a steady stream of smoke flowed from the pipe. He had tried many times to stop smoking but the Doc said if he had to smoke, a pipe was better than anything else. "Yes, Alfie. I talk to him. I don't have enough fingers and toes to count the times I've talked to him. He's real enough, if you want him to be real. It's all in your mind, Alfie. And he's in the mind of those who believe in him. And just about everyone on the Island believes in him. Maybe not as strong as you and I and Sarge do, but things happen that won't let them deny he's out there." They continued their walk in silence.

Alfie stopped at the end of the pier. She looked at the house about two hundred yards away and marveled at its beauty. She would live there one day. She could feel it. "Uncle, will you let me work when I get sixteen?" Uncle Frank laughed. "Ask me when you get sixteen."

The summer was beautiful. Gussie seemed to turn into a woman overnight. Her job at the Clam Digger was working out great and Bunny had already asked her to work next summer. As for Alfie, well she was doing what she loved, helping her Uncle on his fishing boats. Almost wishing she was a boy. She was often mistaken for one, with her short hair and lean frame. As a boy she would be able to go on the long fishing trips. Because of being a girl, she was limited to just the one day trips. And the crew treated her as a lady instead of one of the crew. She thought about Gussie's new boyfriend, Lou. Things surely were getting serious between them. She wondered how Uncle Frank would handle that. She had no doubt but that Gussie would have her way. It was at the clamdigger that Gussie met Lou. It was love at first sight. Lou had flown all the way from Texas to the mainland and then taken a boat to Pink Shell Island, to get away from work,relax and just be himself. But once he saw Gussie he knew his life was about to change. He spent as much time with her as possible, and he grew to love her family almost as much as he loved her. And Uncle Frank and Aunt Kathy thought Lou was teriffic,.

chapter three

THE WEDDING

ALFIE WATCHED AS AUNT Kathy pinned the hem of Gussie's wedding dress up. Uncle Frank stood in the arch of the bedroom door, his pipe hanging loosely from the corner of his mouth, unlit. "What's wrong with everybody," Gussie said. "You would think someone died. I'm getting married. Isn't anyone happy for me?" Uncle Frank removed the pipe from his mouth and crossed the room taking Gussie in his arms. "We are happy for you. We just hate the thought of your moving. Texas is a long way away." Aunt Kathy put the sewing basket away. "Stop making her feel guilty for wanting to leave the Island, Frank. Not everyone loves it like you and Alfie. If I didn't love you so much, I'd leave too." Aunt Kathy walked over to Frank and kissed him on the cheek. "Come on. Let's eat lunch. I made a big pot of dumplings with lobster."

Alfie picked at her food. She was thinking of Guy, the boy she had met on the pier yesterday. Such a strange meeting. Uncle Frank interrupted her thoughts. "You aren't eating, Pumpkin. What's wrong?" "She's never been a big eater. But lobster's your favorite. Alfie, aren't you hungry?" Aunt Kathy had put her fork down and started refilling everyone's iced tea glasses. Everything seemed so hectic these days. No one ever really waited for an answer when they asked a question. Gussie looked over at Alfie. "Maybe she feels a little bit ignored. After all, we don't exactly have a normal routine around here lately. Is that the way you feel, honey? Why don't you and I do something together on my day off, Okay?" She waited for Alfie to answer. "Sure, that would be great. But won't Lou be down?" Alfie knew her sister was just trying to be nice. But she really didn't feel ignored. "You're not getting married for eight months. We have plenty of time to do things together. Anyway, I'm busy helping Sarge mend all of his old fishing nets and fix up his houseboat so we can sleep on it this summer. I love sleeping on the water." "I swear," Gussie said, "you should have been a mermaid." Everyone laughed, including Alfie.

Since meeting Guy Alfie's days were spent trying to be where ever he was.. And for the first time in her life she was totally glad she was a girl. She didn't know what love between a man and woman really was, but she knew she loved Guy. To him, she was a pretty little girl to like, but much too young for romance. But he was pleased she followed him around asking a million questions. The months passed quickly and soon it was one week before the wedding. Everyone was busy and pre-occupied. Gussie was torn and it showed. Alfie, standing out of her way, watched Gussie pack her personal belongings. The more she packed, the more the tears ran down her cheeks. Alfie stood gazing down at the hardwood floor, rubbing the bedpost as if she were summoning a genie, and fighting back tears of her own, managed to say "Geez, if you're feeling so bad, you don't have to get married you know".

Gussie walked over and sat down on the edge of the bed. She pulled Alfie down beside her and into the circle of her arms. "Yes, I have to, Baby. Because I love him so much, I don't think I could live without him. You'll understand what I mean one day. I'm crying because I hate to leave you more than anybody else. I'll miss Uncle Frank and Aunt Kathy, but not the way I'll miss you. Lou said you could come and live with us. I wish you would. You know he's rich, Alfie. He has a big house with maids and cooks that wait on you hand and foot. He has a hundred oil wells or more. I forget now how many he said, but you would live like a princess. Would you like that, Baby?" Alfie reached for a tissue on the nightstand and blew her nose. "I can't leave here, Gussie. I love the Island the way you love Lou. I don't think I could live anywhere else. But I'll come to visit you as often as I can."

The sisters hugged each other for a long time.

The wedding took place on a stretch of flat lava rock close to the ocean. The sea was calm and the waves rolled in one after the other in a silent splendor, as if respecting the vows that were being exchanged. Gussie's soft ivory dress moved with the breeze, reminding Alfie of the wings of a seagull drifting in the ocean air. To Alfie, it was the most beautiful wedding in the world. A look was exchanged between the two sisters and unspoken words were relayed. "Alfie, I had my wedding here just for you", Gussie said, In response, Alfie replied, "I know, thank you". Alfie missed Gussie more than she imagined was ever possible. The loneliness was eased only by phoning each other once a week.

chapter four

FEELINGS

WITH GUSSIE GONE, ALFIE could feel herself changing. She felt older, she wasn't a little girl any longer. Guy became very important to Alfie during the months that stretched ahead. Alfie didn't quite understand the feelings she had about Guy. She knew she missed him terribly when he wasn't around and that her stomach felt like jelly when she saw him. Guy was like a member of the family. Uncle Frank thought he was great, not to mention the fact that he was Kane's nephew. Will was a great fisherman and had one of the best crews of men on the Island. You had to be good to top him. And Kane had certainly gained Uncle Will's respect. Just that alone was enough to get Guy V.I.P. treatment. Guy loved the family. Alfie was like the little sister he never had.

At fourteen, Alfie looked twelve. She hated it. Her body was small and under-developed when compared to those of the other girls her age. Guy was seventeen and was spending more of his time on his uncle's fishing boats. After all, one day they would belong to him. He was one of the best looking men on the Island and had no trouble getting his share of attention from any girl he wanted. Alfie's insides were always in a turmoil every time she heard that Guy was dating someone. The big blow up came when he brought one of his girlfriends to her house, to meet the family. Alfie was so upset she jumped up from the table knocking her bowl of soup over with her elbow as she turned. She could feel her face flush as she ran upstairs into her bedroom and locked the door. She wouldn't even open it for her uncle. She finally let Aunt Kathy in and cried in her arms for an hour. Aunt Kathy knew how she felt. She didn't think Alfie was acting like a baby. Her Uncle Frank had said she was. That alone crushed Alfie. Crushed as only a young girl can be, she hated her Uncle and the Island. And for the first time since arriving she thought of leaving the place most dear to her heart. Guy came over and tried to talk to her. He told her how much she meant to him. He took her in his arms and tried to console her. Her body trembled at his touch. She forgave him.

The next couple of months were great. Guy took Alfie with him everywhere. They laughed and talked the way they had before. There were long walks on the beach and they both talked to the `Old Man in the Sea'. Alfie confessed to him one night while they walked on the beach just how much she loved him. He told her she was still too young, but that he loved her too, and when she was older, maybe things would be different. He told her that his love for her was more like a love for a sister. Alfie's heart seemed to shatter into a million pieces. A sister to Guy was the last thing she wanted to be. Things became strained between them. Soon Guy was dating again and one girl pretty steadily. It was heartbreaking and Alfie tried to avoid seeing him as much as she could. For diversion, she spent a lot of time on Sarge's houseboat. But as hard as she tried, and as much as she wanted to enjoy the sea and all the surroundings on Pink Shell Island, the thought of Guy with another girl would not let the old happiness return.

chapter five

GUY AND JERRY

Guy Eugene Easterman, born May 17, 1943 and Jerry Lee Easterman, born February 7, 1940, were at the ages of three years and three months, they were abandoned on the doorstep of Our Lady of Guadeloupe Church in Mexico City, with their birth certificates pinned to the waistband of Jerry's ragged shorts. The fate or whereabouts of their parents was never discovered. Their birth certificates established that they were born in Dallas, Texas. The small boys were placed in the care of the Sisters until the proper authorities in Dallas made arrangements for the boys to be flown back and placed in the County orphanage.

Guy, a nervous colicky baby, grew into a nervous, thin little boy. He held on to his brother as if his life depended on it. He lived in fear of being punished for small mistakes which he sometimes made, such as spilling his milk or putting his shoes sideways under the bed instead of the uniform way the nuns had instructed them to do it. He would stand with his eyes closed as the nuns made him hold his hands out and the ruler cracked the back of his knuckles ten times on each hand. The tears would spill down his cheeks, streaking his face and sending Jerry into a rage because he had not been around to prevent it. Jerry would always take the blame for Guy, knowing he could take the punishment better. Jerry vowed to find a way out of the orphanage for them.

Jerry was too tall, too thin, and much too old for his age. Sometimes he wished he had never been born, but he wondered then, who would take care of Guy? Jerry's heart would break as he watched Guy stand at the gates of the orphanage and stare at the children passing by with their Moms and Dads. He knew Guy, like himself, was wondering how it would feel to have a family and how it would feel not to have pains in your stomach from being hungry all the time. Jerry was always saving part of his food for Guy because he felt that Guy needed it more than he did.

The boys attended Mass every day along with the other kids in the orphanage, and Jerry knew, deep in his heart, that there was a God even though none of his prayers were ever answered. He felt that maybe he was too bad. There was definitely something wrong. But faith that God would one day hear him kept him going. Jerry tore pieces of cardboard from one of the trash boxes and put them in the insides of their shoes. At least that would keep the water out. He buttoned Guy's worn, thin sweater up around his neck. Guy was coughing a lot lately and the cough syrup the

Sisters gave him didn't seem to help. He had asked the Sister in charge to let Guy see a doctor, but the Sister had laughed at him. "A doctor," she said. "Why we can't even get enough food or clothes for you and you think the county will okay a doctor to see your brother." She laughed again. "You poor boy." Jerry's bewildered gaze must have touched the Sister's heart, because she walked over to him and laid her hand on his shoulder. "Do you think we like to see you children suffer the way you do. But no one listens to our needs so we just gave up asking. But I'll see if I can get some stronger medicine for your brother, okay?" She patted his head and walked away.

The Sister kept her word and a better medicine was given to Guy, and for a while he seemed to get better. And time passed, with very little change inside the orphanage. At nine years of age, Guy was still sickly and the twelve year old Jerry was still doing everything possible for his younger brother. This particular winter seemed to be colder than any Jerry could ever remember. The old gas heaters used to heat the orphanage hardly did the job when working, and in their current state of ill repair, no one could stay warm. Guy was thinner than he had ever been, and his skin had taken on a yellow look. A continuous cough shook his small, thin frame. He ached all over, especially his head and neck. He woke one morning burning with fever. He couldn't move his neck. The pain was terrible. He wondered how he could get Jerry's attention. His cot was next to Jerry's but it might as well have been a mile away. The tears made their way down his face. He hated himself for always crying. Jerry never cried. Jerry swung his feet over the side of the narrow cot that served as a bed and shivered from the cold. He reached for his shirt and slipped it over his pajama top. His toes felt cramped inside the to-short shoes. Another month and he wouldn't be able to get them on. He dreaded the long day ahead. If it weren't for Guy, he would walk out the door and keep walking. Jerry looked over to Guy's cot. Guy's face was flushed red from the fever and tears of pain rolled steadily down his cheeks. Jerry's screams could be heard throughout the orphanage. In seconds, the Sisters were next to Guy's cot.

Sister Cora, the Sister in charge, the same one who had arranged to get Guy better cough medicine, now made arrangements to have Guy taken to County General Hospital. Jerry was not allowed to go. The only real affection they had ever received, other than the love they had given each other, was from Sister Arlina. She was their teacher and counselor at the orphanage. Her heart had always gone out to these two boys. The bond of love between them was stronger than any she had ever witnessed in her years of teaching there. She had always managed extra time to help them with their studies. They were both quick learners and retained what they had learned. When they finished their studies, she would slip them fruit, and hug them close as she whispered words of comfort, telling them that soon conditions in the orphanage would improve, or that one day someone would choose to take them home. She would cry after they left, thinking of their frail bodies and the world of these poor orphans. She would light extra candles for the boys when she went to Mass. She prayed for God to watch over them.

It was Sister Arlina who came over to Jerry to comfort him when they took Guy away. She could feel the pain inside Jerry as she hugged him close. He buried his face in the Sister's cape. The lump was so big in his throat from holding back tears he felt he would choke. But he couldn't cry, Guy needed him to be strong. He lifted his head. His eyes locked with the Sister's. He said, "Sister Arlina, please help me get to the hospital. Guy's never been anywhere without me before. He's probably scared to death. Please, Sister." Sister Arlina knew if she didn't help him he would find a way without her.

chapter six
───────────

THE MIRACLE

SISTER ARLINA WALKED TO the old '37 Chevy with Jerry close behind her. Jerry sat in the front seat next to the Sister. His heart pounded in his chest. He could think of nothing but Guy. If Guy died, he knew he would die too. Sister Arlina sensed that Jerry did not want to talk. She patted his hand reassuringly. Jerry was grateful for the silence. Jerry had never been in a hospital. Every thing was clean and white. Nurses in their starched white uniforms were every where. Sister Arlina went up to the information booth as Jerry stood by the door. She came back and took Jerry's arm, guiding him toward the elevators. They got off on the seventh floor. A long hallway loomed before them. The floor glistened with wax. Signs hung in the hallway over each door. Jerry read them as they walked - Laboratory, Pathology, Internist, X-Ray, Gerald Robbins, M. D., Resident Doctor.

Sister Arlina stopped in front of Dr. Robbins' door. They entered the office. The Sister motioned for Jerry to sit down as she walked to the receptionist's window. The Sister was led into an office that was crammed with furniture. Expensive dark brown leather chairs and a leather sofa with massive tan-colored lamps made the office look small. Certificates lined three of the four walls. A tall handsome man of medium build and height entered the office. His hair was almost white, and his skin was bronzed from the sun. He smiled, flashing white, even teeth. Sister Arlina noticed his long slim fingers and immaculate nails as he extended his hand to her. "Hello. I'm Dr. Robbins and you're Sister"? he waited for her to reply. "I'm Sister Arlina. I'm the teacher and counselor for the children at the orphanage. I'm here to see about Guy Easterman. I understand that you're his doctor."

Dr. Robbins looked into the Sister's eyes. "Guy is a very sick child. He has spinal meningitis. Not to mention the fact he is undernourished and has needed medical attention long before now. Tell me, Sister, doesn't the orphanage provide a resident doctor for the children? The County surely supplies the money for one. Is the young lad sitting in the waiting room Guy's brother?" "Yes, Doctor, he is Guy's brother. His name is Jerry. And Doctor, I don't know what the County supplies for the children. I'm not in charge of the finances there. I do know that conditions in the orphanage are bad and have steadily grown worse." "I'd like to examine Jerry while he's here, if that's all right with you? Of course, there will be no charge for it."

The doctor knew that Jerry was near tears. He put his arm around Jerry's shoulders and said, "Let's go see your brother. You know he's going to be all right." The doctor stopped walking and looked down into Jerry's face. "Well, you do believe that, don't you?" The doctor waited for Jerry to answer. "Well?" the doctor said. "Yes, sir. I believe it," Jerry's voice quivered with emotion."Good," the doctor said. "I believe it, too."

Sister Arlina followed the doctor and Jerry. The wards were filled with twenty beds each. Ten on each side of the room. Guy's bed was the last one on the left side next to the window. A white screen surrounded his bed giving an illusion of privacy. The doctor pulled the screen back making room for Jerry to enter. Guy's eyes were closed. He opened them as Jerry reached the side of his bed. He tried to smile. Jerry reached for his hand and held it tight. The lump in Jerry's throat was unreal. He had never cried in his life and now he could hardly hold the tears back. His voice quivered as he spoke. "You're going to be okay. You believe that, don't you?" Tears slid down Guy's cheek as Jerry spoke. If he lost Guy, he would have no one. "Just say you believe it. Just shake your head yes." He wiped Guy's eyes with a handkerchief the doctor had handed him. Guy shook his head yes. Jerry felt like a weight had been lifted from his shoulders. He knew now that Guy would get well. The doctor finished his examination of Jerry, concluding that although he was severely undernourished like his brother and in need of dental work, he was otherwise perfectly healthy. He thought, to himself, "It's amazing what punishment the human body can take."

The doctor led Jerry and the Sister to the hospital cafeteria. Jerry's eyes grew big as he took in the hot food and the rows of pie and cake. He had never seen food like this in his life. The doctor said, "You can have anything you want. We're celebrating." Jerry looked puzzled as the doctor continued. "I've never had a family. I've often thought of having one, but I was always so busy and I don't know what kind of parent I'll be, but Guy needs someplace besides that orphanage if he's ever going to get well. Why don't I make arrangements for you and your brother to spend the next few weeks at my home, that is if you want to?"

Jerry thought he must be dreaming. No one had ever wanted them before. This was the first time the boys had been separated. It seemed odd that the only thoughts running through Jerry's head right now were about the times that families had come to the orphanage to select children which they wanted to adopt, and not one time, over all the years, had one family ever picked them. Not one time. What a thing to think about at a time like this, Jerry thought. He couldn't believe what he had heard.

"You want me and my brother to come and live with you? Me and my brother? You want us?" The doctor put his hand on Jerry's arm and said, "Yes, I do. We'll see how things work out. Okay with you?" "You bet it's okay with me. You bet it is." Jerry had a grin on his face that went from ear to ear. Sister Arlina had started to cry. "You don't know how long I've prayed for something like this to happen to these boys. God has answered my prayers." "And mine, too," Jerry said to himself. "And mine, too."

The doctor made arrangements with the orphanage to have Guy and Jerry released to him. He also contacted the State authorities and reported the conditions that existed at the orphanage. He learned from Sister Arlina, thanks to him, the children in the orphanage were now living in better conditions. There was enough food for all, and each child was given adequate clothing to meet each season of the year. The antiquated heaters were replaced and each bed had a pillow and a warm blanket. The blankets were donated by Dr. Robbins himself. He also insisted that proper medical and dental care be given to every child.

For Jerry and Guy, the weeks ahead surpassed any dreams that the boys could ever have had. The doctor's good care transformed the once frail boys into a picture of health. The Doctor took pride in the remarkable changes the boys made as he introduced them to tennis, horseback riding, and deep sea fishing. The doctor insisted that the boys call him Doc, as a deep bond formed between the three, leaving no doubt in the Doctor's mind that the boys were meant to share his life. As Guy and Jerry sat in the deep red leather chairs of the lawyer's office, they knew that they loved the tall distinguished white haired man that stood before them. As the lawyer handed him a pen and said, "Sign all six copies, Gerald." The gates of Davey Jones locker opened freeing the boys at last as the Doc signed the last paper.

Jerry took great pride in his new home, overseeing the care of Doc's thoroughbred stallion and roaming the vast acres of the ranch with Coco, the gold and white palomino mare Doc had given him. The smell of pine filled his nostrils as he pulled Coco's reins gently bringing the palomino to a stop. The palomino snorted as she raised her hoof up and down hitting the soft mound of dirt under the massive pine tree. Jerry thought of Guy and how their closeness had slowly been divided by Jerry's love for the ranch and Guy's love for the sea. Guy would finish his chores at the ranch early and the rest of the day was spent with doc's half brother Will, Doc's only living relative. Will had been a fisherman all of his life and now owned his own fishing boats on Pink Shell Island. Will had taught Guy to fish and master Doc's twenty-five foot sailboat. Guy knew he too wanted to be a fisherman. Uncle Will had come to visit two months ago and had stayed. He had been lonely on the Island. His wife had been dead for three years. The boys made him feel young again. He knew he would miss them when he went home.

Thia put the last steak on the barbecue. Jerry thought she was the most beautiful woman he had ever seen. He wondered what it would be like to touch her soft, ivory skin. He had a pang of guilt for having the thought. He must be mad. Thia was the Doc's girlfriend. There was no better person in the world than the Doc. He looked at Thia's long red hair and red full mouth as his body ached to hold her. Geez, what was wrong with him lately?

His face reddened as Thia's eyes met his and traveled down his naked chest to his swimming trunks. She smiled and turned her attention back to the steaks. Her small firm body pushed to free itself from the to tight strapless short set.

Geez, Jerry thought, was she flirting with him? She had only been seeing the Doc for a couple of weeks. Jerry's fifteen-year-old body was that of a man's. He was muscular and lean and ready. Thia was only ten years older than Jerry and thirty one years younger than the Doc. The Doc always went with the younger women. He'd never had time for marriage and he didn't look even close to his fifty-five years. Oh, well, Jerry thought. The Doc wouldn't have Thia for a girlfriend long if her eyes were already roving. It was just as well. The Doc deserved someone who appreciated him.

Doc walked out the patio doors carrying drinks in tall frosted glasses. Will and Guy by his side. Guy and Uncle Will were already deep in conversation. Guy looked up and caught Jerry's questioning eyes. Guy said, "Uncle Will wants us to go and stay with him this summer. Man, I can hardly wait." Uncle Will grinned as his pipe dangled from the corner of his mouth. "That's right, and that includes Doc. I never thought I'd have one nephew and now I've got two." He walked over to Jerry and patted him on the back. "You boys have been like a tonic to me. I feel mighty lucky."

Guy and Uncle Will soon became inseparable. Guy would sit for hours listening to one story after another about fishing and the sea. Jerry had enough after one day. But as the months passed Uncle Will's visits became more frequent and his stay longer each time. And Thia was still in Doc's life. She came and went interested only in the beautiful gifts Doc gave her. But that seemed all that Doc wanted too. The doctor was putting in long hours and had started to expand his offices. He had taken on two associates as his patients continued to multiply. The doctor had given up his residence at the hospital soon after adopting the boys. Now just two years later his practice was too large for him to handle it alone.

Jerry sat alone out by the pool. Why hadn't he taken Bonnie out? Every boy in school wanted her and she wanted Jerry. She had made it quite obvious lately. She went out of her way to talk to him and even offered to help him with his algebra. But she seemed so immature. He wanted a woman. Guy and Uncle Will had gone to a movie. Doc had been called to the hospital, emergency surgery on one of his gall bladder patients. Maybe he would shower and head down to the movies. He hadn't exactly been the best company lately to Uncle Will. He started to get up when the patio door slid open. Thia stood in the doorway. Her short shorts and halter top left little to the imagination. "Hi. Where's Doc? Are you here alone?" Jerry dove into the pool. There was no other way to hide the embarrassment that engulfed his young manhood. He swam the length of the pool under the water. He wanted her to leave, he surfaced. Thia was standing on the side of the pool her scanty shorts and halter top lay next to her feet. She sat on the side and slid into the water. Jerry was holding his breath. His heart pounded within his chest so hard he was sure she could hear it..She led him to the shallow end.of the pool. Her hands on his skin felt like burning coals. He had never felt like this in his life. Time and sound stood still as Thia kissed his ear.

The good feeling was gone as Jerry sat in the dark of his room. The guilt feelings engulfing him like the night. Jerry heard the front door open. He heard Guy call his name. The light knock on his bedroom door. Soon the foot steps went away. He heard the phone ring. The front door opened and closed. There were no more sounds. He went downstairs. He wondered why Guy and Uncle Will had left again. He turned on the lamp in the den. There was a note on the coffee table. The note had his name on it. His vision seemed to blurr as he read it. "Jerry, come to the hospital as soon as you can. Doc had a heart attack. Guy." Oh, my God, what had he done. The phone call must have been the hospital calling.

Doc died before Jerry could reach the hospital. Guy was in a daze when Jerry arrived. The tears in his eyes were not as they once had been when he was a small frightened boy, but the emotional tears of a man that had lost a person he truly loved. Jerry felt numb. He felt that he must be losing his mind because a feeling of relief washed over him at the idea that now the Doc would never have to know about him and Thia. He was ashamed. Geez, what was wrong with him? Guy would hate him for the way he was thinking. He hated himself. The Doc's best friend and associate offered to buy the ranch so that the boys could go and live with Uncle Will. Soon, all of the doctor's affairs were in order and the will was read, leaving everything equally to Jerry and Guy. Uncle Will had been appointed their guardian. Jerry and Guy were both very wealthy young men.

Guy fell in love with the Island, but Jerry mentally made plans to leave. Guy fit right into Uncle Will's life. They were always together. Guy knew more about the fishing industry in six months than most fishermen learned in their entire lives. Uncle Will was almost proud enough to burst. Time passed quickly and soon Jerry was eighteen and legally eligible to receive his inheritance. This was the day he had been waiting for. Jerry had graduated from school with honors. And he knew now that he wanted to be a lawyer. That meant college and there were none on the Island. But first he wanted to travel for a year or so. He talked things over with Uncle Will and Uncle Will knew there was no stopping him.

Jerry hated good-byes. Especially to Guy. He left one day while Guy was still at the boat dock. A letter lay on Guy's dresser. Guy read the letter that evening when he returned home. He had walked past his Uncle and out the patio door with the letter still in his hand. He stood on the deserted pier and cried. He cried for the horrible life they once lived. He cried for Doc. He cried for the angry feeling he felt toward his brother for leaving him. Then he cried because he was thankful for having Uncle Will. He dropped the letter into the ocean.

chapter seven

THE BEGINNING

ALFIE FELT HYPNOTIZED BY the ocean. She watched as the waves rolled in and broke before they reached the shore. Thoughts of Guy flooded her mind like a giant tidal wave. When did the hurt stop and the healing begin. It had been two years and she still felt as if someone had just poured salt into an open wound. She closed her eyes as she lay her head back against the soft chaise lounge.

Her mind raced back in time. She was twelve years old again. She saw herself walking on the pier... The fog was heavy today. She knew Uncle Frank would say no if she asked to go out on the fishing boats. Darn, that meant another day helping Aunt Kathy in the house. Maybe she could call Gussie and ask if it would be okay to go and visit them for a couple of days. She looked around for old Sarge. It was then that she heard the crying. Who was it? She spotted a figure leaning against the rail of the pier. She stopped and stared. She wanted to move but her legs felt frozen . She had never seen anyone cry like that before. The crying stopped. The figure turned. Alfie recognized him. He went to the same school she did. The boy wiped his eyes with the back of his sleeve. His eyes locked with hers. She could see the embarrassment in his eyes. Then anger seemed to twist the shape of his handsome face. His mouth opened. "What are you staring at, you little brat? Can't a person have a little privacy. Go on, get outta here."

Alfie's lips quivered. A yell escaped her as she turned and ran up the pier. She started to cry. The tears blinded her as she ran. She heard someone running behind her shouting for her to stop. She ran even faster. She felt a hand on her arm and she was turned to face the same tall figure she had run from. "Hey, I'm sorry. I didn't mean to scare you." He handed Alfie his handkerchief. She wiped her eyes. "Are you okay," he said. "Yeah. I'm okay. Are you?" Alfie looked into the bluest eyes she had ever seen. His hair was the color of wheat and his skin was bronzed from the sun. He smiled as he ruffled her hair with his hand.

"Why, you're just a kid. I've seen you around school, sixth grade, right?" She would have given anything for him to be wrong. She said, "Yes, but I'm not a kid." With his hand on her arm, he guided her off the pier. "I live right over there." He pointed to a house that sat about two hundred yards from the pier. "My name is Guy. What's yours?" The house he pointed to was Alfie's dream house on the Island. She had always said that one day she would live there. The house was built from redwood and brick with a patio almost surrounding it. It had a look of elegance, or, as her uncle would have said, "old money." "I love that house," Alfie said. "Yeah. Actually, it belongs to my uncle. I guess it is pretty nice. He's not really my uncle. It's a long story. You see, I was adopted." Soon he was pouring out his life story to her. And, in turn, she told him hers. A confidence formed as they talked. Alfie felt she had known him forever. Alfie seemed to fill the void Jerry had left in Guy's life. A sister. A friend. Guy felt that he could tell Alfie almost anything.

Alfie had a hard time trying to understand the feelings she had toward Guy. It was Aunt Kathy who finally helped Alfie sort things out. Alfie worked fiendishly as she polished the furniture with lemon oil. Anyone caught setting a glass down on these tables would answer to her. She pictured herself with her foot resting on the body of a faceless figure. She had a sword in her hand with the tip pressed against the throat of the faceless figure who was pleading with her for forgiveness and promising to polish the table forever if she would spare him. Aunt Kathy's voice startled Alfie from her daydream. Her arm hit the bottle of lemon oil, and it went flying to the floor. The yellow liquid poured from the neck of the bottle and Alfie burst into tears. Aunt Kathy hurried to Alfie's side and gathered her into her arms. "There now. Don't cry. It's only furniture polish. I'll help you clean it up. No harm done." "Oh, Aunt Kathy, I hate boys! I hate them! They mess up everything, All they care about is their own feelings, why"? She twisted from Aunt Kathy's arms and ran to her room.

Alfie tried to ignore the gentle tapping on the door as she closed her eyes and imagined herself running through a field of bright yellow daisies. The daisies stopped at the edge of a hill that led down to the ocean. She sat down letting her feet dangle over the side. The ocean seemed to ease the hurt feeling inside her; the daisies gave her a feeling of being free. Their softness cushioned her head as she drifted into a land of pink and blue fluffy clouds. Aunt Kathy spread the soft comforter up over her shoulders. Alfie opened her eyes. Aunt Kathy sat on the side of her bed. "Does he know how you feel about him?" Aunt Kathy brushed the hair back from her forehead.

chapter eight

THE DECISION

THE MONTHS AHEAD WERE busy ones for Alfie. She had finally realized that her feelings for Guy needed to be kept in a small compartment of her heart and released at the right time. She would know when that time came. She had taken a job helping Sarge collect the beautiful pink shells on the Island and turning them into lamps and ash trays. These were sold in a room that was attached to Sarge's house. Sarge's house sat on the beach and was easily seen by the tourists who flocked to the small Island throughout the year in an attempt to escape the busy life on the mainland. Alfie loved the work at Sarge's shell shop. Her shell designs for birds, especially the seagulls and pelicans had nearly doubled Sarge's sales.

Alfie's small, thin frame remained the same. Instead of looking fifteen she looked twelve. Only now, she didn't worry about it. When Guy called she had Aunt

Kathy tell him that she was out. She heard enough about his girl friends from the other girls in school. She didn't need to hear about them from him, and she was sure that's what he wanted to tell her whenever he called. Alfie had decided that Guy wouldn't tell her about his love life anymore because she wouldn't listen. Alfie always made excuses when he tried to talk to her at school. She ignored the hurt look on his face, never once thinking that he might want to talk to her because he missed her and the closeness that they had shared. The problem was she missed him, too. Maybe that's why she found herself standing next to the pier, looking at the house that sat two hundred yards away, as her heart softened and her feet carried her in the direction she wanted to go.

She knocked softly on the front door. She had started to leave when she heard laughter from inside. She walked to the side patio door and stuck her head in. She had almost called out when her eyes rested on a tall, curvy figure which had her arms twisted so tightly around Guy's body that it was a wonder he could even breathe. The tall, blond girl said, "What are you waiting for?" She giggled as her mouth found Guy's. Alfie's hand flew to her mouth as she stifled a sob. She ran home as if the hounds of Hell were after her. Her chest ached as she flew into her room and slammed the door. She knew the ache in her chest was not from running. She was grateful that no one was home to hear the sobs that echoed throughout the house.

When Aunt Kathy came home Alfie was packing her suitcase. Aunt Kathy stood at the bedroom door.

She looked as if she might cry any second. "Have you talked to your Uncle? Whatever has happened, I'm sure it can be resolved if we just talk." The sides of the suitcase bulged as Alfie set it on the floor. Alfie walked over to Aunt Kathy, put her arms around her neck and cried. Aunt Kathy cried with her. The airport was crowded as Alfie waited in the ticket line. She felt a hand on her arm. She turned and stared into the blue eyes of Guy. Her heart melted as he smiled. "Your uncle told me you were down here. Where are you going?" "I'm not going anywhere today. I'm buying my ticket so I can leave Friday. I'm going to visit Gussie and Lou for a while. Gussie has had surgery and needs my help." "I thought that Lou was loaded. Can't he hire someone?" "Whether he's loaded or not has nothing to do with it. My sister needs me and I'm going. Anyway it's none of your business. Why should you care if I leave or not? What's the matter? Did the tall blond toss you aside?"

Alfie turned and walked up to the ticket window. When she had bought her ticket and looked around, Guy was gone. "Good," she thought as she opened the door of the airport and strolled lazily down the quiet, friendly streets of the Island. She walked along the jetty and searched the rocks for clams. A sadness swept over her, she would miss this place. But she knew she had to get away for awhile. She saw Guy sitting on a rock poking a stick around in the water. She started to turn and run, but her body continued forward against her will. Why should she leave? This was her Island. He was the intruder. He didn't turn his head as he said, "Why are you so mad at me? And how do you know about the blond?" "I know about the blond because I peeked into your patio door and saw her doing a strip for you. And I'm not mad at you. I hate you. Now leave me alone, you creep!" The tears had started down Alfie's cheeks as she turned to run. Guy caught her and spun her around. "What were you doing? Spying on me? What I do is none of your business. You've been treating me like a leper. What do you want from me? You're making my damned life miserable. Did you know that? I thought we were friends. I thought you cared for me the same way that I care for you. Evidently I was wrong. Maybe it would be better if you just stayed out of my life. Just leave me alone." Alfie's feelings of fury subsided as her voice softened and the tears continued slowly down her cheeks. "I don't want to leave you alone. I love you. And all you think about me is that I'm a child. I'm fifteen. Can't you see I'm not a child any longer? Are you blind to everyone's feelings and wants but your own?"

Guy crushed Alfie to him and kissed her forehead. "Oh my sweet Alfie. I'm so sorry, so sorry. Can you forgive me for being such an idiot? I love you too. But I'm to old for you. I'll soon be twenty Your Uncle would never approve of our dating. Not yet, anyway. We have our whole lives ahead of us. Can't you wait awhile?" Alfie twisted from his arms and ran. This time Guy didn't try to stop her. Alfie boarded the plane, an aura of great loss engulfed her. Not even thoughts of seeing Gussie could make her feel better. She lay her head back and let sleep claim her thoughts.

chapter nine

DALLAS

ALFIE'S EYES WIDENED AS she looked around the Dallas Airport. She spotted Lou. He was wearing a cream colored western cut suit with a Stetson hat to match. His brown shirt and brown alligator boots gave him a distinguished look of "old money." His Tampa cigar singed her hair as he grabbed her in a big bear hug. He pushed her away from him. "My, my. You sure have grown up. Why you're plum pretty. I bet all them boys on the Island follow you around like a puppy dog." He hugged Alfie again as his big bull head-shaped diamond ring scratched her cheek. Lou was a tall, handsome man with leathery brown skin and jet black hair. He smelled of Poco Raban.

Lou seemed to know everyone as they made their way through the crowded airport. The skycap ran to help with the luggage. Lou patted the young man on the back as he said, "Why, Ronnie Lee, how are you doing, boy? Heard your mama is under the weather. This here is my sister-in-law Alfie. Say hey to Ronnie Lee, Alfie. She's here to stay for awhile. I'm gonna be having a party or two. I'll give your family a ring." Lou peeled off a ten from a roll of bills he pulled from his pocket and tucked it into Ronnie Lee's hand. "Thank you Mr. Phillips. I'll tell my folks you're gonna call. Tell Mrs. Phillips we all hope she's felling better and that if there's anything we can do just call. It was nice meeting you Alfie." Ronnie Lee put the luggage in the trunk of the long, white Cadillac. He smiled and waved as they pulled away from the curb.

The Cadillac wound it's way through the wide streets of Dallas. The buildings were massive. Alfie felt small and unimportant. She missed Pink Shell Island already. Soon the tall buildings were behind them and suddenly oil wells were everywhere. Lou had been talking, she hadn't heard a word. "Hey, Alfie are you asleep, Hon?" The long Cadillac swerved from one lane to the other as Lou talked. "See those oil wells over there Alfie?" Lou made a sweeping motion with his hand taking in all the oil wells Alfie could see. "Those are all mine. Ain't that a purty sight?" Lou grinned and stuck his chest out a little farther. Alfie said, "I've never seen so many oil wells. You must be very wealthy.?"

Lou grinned with the big Tampa sticking out of the side of his mouth. "I don't like to brag about how much money I have. Let's just say I won't never starve." He laughed as the big car swerved to the other lane. The wail of a siren sounded behind them.

Lou pulled to the side of the road and turned off the motor. A big burly cop stepped out. The cop and Lou grinned as they pumped each others hand up and down. "How you doing, Clyde? I'm sure glad you stopped me. I got those fight tickets you wanted." Lou reached into his inside coat pocket and pulled out some tickets. "I stopped you to find out how Gussie's doing. I forgot all about them tickets. I called out to your house several times but Gussie's always sleeping and you ain't never there. What are you trying to do, work yourself to death." Clyde pulled a cigar from his shirt pocket and bit the end off. "Naw, I ain't working that hard. Trent's taken over most of the work load. He's a good man. But then I make it worth his while." "I'm just coming from the airport." He poked his head through the car window. "Clyde, this-here is my sister-in-law, Alfie. Alfie, this-here is Clyde. He's the police chief of Dallas. Alfie's gonna stay with us a spell. I think she's just what the doctor ordered for Gussie."

Clyde's cigar hit the side of the window as he poked his head inside the car. "Pleased to meet you Alfie. We'll have you over to the house before you leave. I've got a boy about your age that would do cartwheels to have a purty girl like you around." Clyde's wide grin showed his one gold tooth. "I'm gonna give a party or two while Alfie's here. I'll call you and Ethel. I'll tell Gussie you asked about her."

A tall white wall loomed up ahead of them. The wall surrounded an old colonial white house. The porch was supported by marble pillars. The car turned into the winding driveway and Lou stopped at the double wrought iron gates. Lou stuck his arm out and put a key into a small electronic latch on the side of the gate. The gates slowly opened. Alfie turned in her seat and watched the gates close behind them. The car circled the driveway and stopped in front of the mansion.

A butler opened the door and hurried down the stairs tipping his hat as he smiled. His white teeth made his dark skin look even darker. "I'm glad you're home, Mr. Phillips. I thought Mrs. Phillips was gonna have a nervous breakdown pacing the floor and asking every five seconds if you had called." Lou laughed. "I figured she'd be doing that, Lonnie." Lonnie opened the car door for Alfie. "And this here is what she's been waiting for, ain't it?" He grinned as he helped Alfie from the car. "Welcome to Dallas, Miss Alfie." "Thank you, Lonnie." Alfie liked this old Black man. Alfie looked around at the plush, green, manicured lawn. Old, old money, Alfie thought.

Eppie, the head maid, greeted them at the door. Her skin was the color of milk chocolate. She was meticulously groomed, from the tip of her polished blacked pumps to the top of her soft black curls. She smiled a soft, warm smile as she greeted Alfie and took her linen jacket and purse and handed them to another maid that stood on the side waiting to take any order that Eppie gave. Her stern, yet soft, voice made Lonnie jump as he stood grinning at the bottom of the stairs. "Lonnie, did you forget what you'er supposed to be doing? The luggage, Lonnie. The luggage." She turned toward Alfie. "Your things will be put in your room. Sarah will be your personal maid." A young black girl seemed to appear from nowhere, her skin the same milk chocolate color as Eppie's. "Thank you." Alfie said. Lou had disappeared. Alfie looked at the shinning marble floor, the different colored statues, and the vases of flowers that sat on every polished table as far as the eye could see. It was so beautiful.

"It's about time you got here." Alfie looked up and saw Gussie walking down the winding staircase with the dark, cranberry carpet sinking under each step she took. Gussie wore a flowing robe of emerald green silk with matching mule slippers. Her long, blond hair was pulled up into a soft bun. She looked like a painting. Alfie ran to meet her. The girls embraced. They were crying and laughing at the same time. "I'm so glad you're here. So glad." Gussie blew her nose. Alfie said, "So am I, it's hard to believe I'm really here. We've got a lot to talk about. Are you okay? What kind of surgery did you have?" Alfie hugged Gussie again. Gussie put her arm around Alfie's shoulder and led her back up the stairs. "First, lets get you settled and then we'll talk. I'll bet you're exhausted." Alfie's maid followed close behind with a tall, cold pitcher of lemonade.

Alfie's room was decorated in caramel and soft pink. Alfie and Gussie spent the entire afternoon curled up in identical lounge chairs of soft pink silk. They talked and laughed about everyone and everything from the past up until the very moment they sipped their lemonade and ate the thinly sliced cucumber and avocado finger sandwiches. "I can't believe you would have such a serious operation and not tell any of us. You said it was minor surgery. We would have been here with you. Uncle Frank and Aunt Kathy will be furious when they find out." Alfie's voice couldn't hide the hurt as she scolded Gussie. "Alfie, calm down. I would have told you, but I didn't know myself. I went into the hospital to have a cyst removed and when I woke up they had removed my whole breast." Gussie dabbed at a tear that slid from the corner of her eye.

"Oh, honey, don't cry. I can just imagine what you've been through. I just wish I could have been here with you. Are you going to be all right? I mean, is that all the surgery they're going to do?" Alfie shivered at the thought of having only one breast. Poor Gussie. "I hope so. When they took my breast they put a silicone one in its place, so I still have a breast. I just have to go in for checkups every three months for the first two years. That's to make sure no more lumps form. And, if they do, they can catch them right away. I have one of the best doctors in Dallas. He said I have nothing to worry about." Gussie yawned. Sarah pulled the soft wool-blended afghans over the girls and closed the drapes.

Alfie walked into the dining room. Gussie and Lou had just started to eat their soup. Lou stood up as the maid seated Alfie. "We thought we'd let you sleep.

You looked like you needed it. Remember, if you ever miss a meal around here, we have a cook on duty at all times who will fix anything you can think of at any time of the day or night." One maid dipped artichoke and oyster soup into Alfie's bowl, while another filled her wine glass.

Alfie was satisfied as they left the doctor's office. Gussie's doctor was excellent. He had taken the time to sit down and explain, in layman's talk, exactly what Gussie had gone through and what she could expect in the future. He had given Gussie the green light on all activities as long as she didn't overdo it. The girls headed for the Galleria, one of the largest and finest shopping malls in Dallas. Gussie was excited about their shopping together. Gussie pulled Alfie into Victoria's and they buried themselves in nighties. Alfie drooled as she slipped the ivory satin gown over her head. This was great, she thought, as they paid the clerk for six gowns and robes. After two hours of trying on shoes, Alfie could see that Gussie was tired,she said "Let's go. We can shop every day if we want to." She wound her arm through Gussie's as they made their way through the crowd. The girls laid their heads back on the cool leather seats as the chauffeur drove them home.

The girls lay by the pool. Suntan oil covered their bodies. "It must be 120 degrees out here." Alfie sat up and reached for the iced tea on the patio table. "I think I'll take a quick dip." Wipe some of that oil off before you go in." Gussie turned on her stomach.

The phone rang. Gussie put the receiver to her ear. She smiled as she lay the receiver back down. "That's the fourth call today. Boy, you two must really be in love." Alfie turned onto her back. "He used to call me ten times a day until I accused him of not trusting me. There are phones in every room of the house and in all the cars. Sometimes I think he loves me too much." Gussie sat up and reached for a towel.

"I don't believe you can love someone too much," Alfie said as she wiped the oil from her legs. Gussie looked at Alfie and smiled. "What do you know about being in love? Come on now, tell me. Who are you in love with? Oh my Gawd! I knew it. You are in love. You've been holding out on me, you little rat." She jumped up and popped Alfie with her towel. Alfie squealed and jumped, doing a belly flop into the pool. Gussie doubled over laughing. Alfie pushed herself up on the side of the pool. Gussie sat next to her. "Anyone I know?" Gussie took a sip of tea. "Yes, you know him." Alfie dried her hair as she tried to bury her face in the towel. "Why, you're blushing. I knew the last time Lou and I were on the Island to visit you that you were in love. It's Guy, isn't it?" Gussie hugged Alfie. "How does he feel about it?" "He loves me like a sister. Can you blame him? I mean, look at me. I have the mind of a twenty year old and the body of a ten year old. I know, don't say it. One day I'll wake up and have a woman's body.""Oh, baby, don't feel that way. If a man loves you, he loves you the way you are. If Guy can't see that, well, he doesn't deserve you. And you will start developing soon. I know you will. Some girls just start later than others. You're a very special person and I think Guy is, too. One day he'll see that he loves you more than just sister love."

They went to the beach at least once a week. Alfie missed the ocean. At home all she had to do was walk out of her back door and there it was. She wondered why Lou didn't have a beach home. Several months passed and Alfie noticed that her clothes had begun to feel a lot tighter across the bust and looser in the waist. Great, she thought. I have to put on weight just when I have new clothes. She cut down on eating. It didn't seem to help. Gussie watched the change take place. It was like watching a caterpillar become a butterfly. She didn't say anything to Alfie. She would soon make the discovery for herself.

Alfie stood in front of the bedroom mirror. She ran her hands over her naked body. She placed her two hands around her waist. She could almost touch her fingers together. Her finger circled her nipples, her hands cupped her breasts. They were full and round. She turned sideways. Her round firm buttocks pushed out just enough. Her face was thinner, making her high cheek bones protrude. Her skin was smooth and tan. The body that looked back at her was a woman's body, full and ripe. At breakfast that morning she felt different. She knew her discovery wasn't a secret. She picked at her hot cereal with disinterest. Lou had to leave. He came over and kissed the top of Alfie's head. Then he gave Gussie a long, passionate kiss. Alfie wanted to say something but she didn't know how to start. She looked up at Gussie. Gussie smiled and turned up the palms of her hands. She said, "Walla! It happens overnight. Didn't I tell you?"

chapter ten

THE PARTY

ALFIE WATCHED GUSSIE AS she made out the menu for the up and coming party. There would be at least two hundred guests. Everyone was caught up in the excitement. It had been a long time since a party had been given at the Phillips' estate. The cooks sang as they went about their preparations. Alfie had made out the invitations. She didn't know any of the guests with the exception of a few she had met when she first arrived in Dallas. Gussie told her they were all V.I.P. Alfie's puzzled expression had caused Gussie to laugh. "Very important people" "Oh, like Mr. and Mrs. Jeffery L. Shell. They are no doubt, oil people. My, my. I will be rubbing noses with the elite." Alfie walked with her hand on her hip, her nose in the air.

"Yes, dahling, and don't you forget it. This party is being given for little ol' you. We have to shop for a few new clothes this afternoon. About a dozen or so dresses, does that suit my lady? Gussie made a sweeping bow.Do you Remember a few months after you arrived here you turned 16 and you wouldn't let me do anything for you. So Lou will be spending his money on you and me, don't you love it.""I certainly won't argue with you I love clothes and I think a dozen or so will be just fine that is until we can do some serious shopping." They hugged each other, laughing at their silliness. Alfie had been here almost a year and it only seemed like a few months. where had the time gone, she felt closer to Gussie than she ever had. how could she leave.

The maid brought in the mail. There was a letter for Alfie. It was from Uncle Frank. Disappointment covered her face. She had expected a letter from Guy. She tore the letter open. It was the usual news. Oh, Guy's Uncle Will was ill. In fact he had been in the hospital for a week. Guy was staying busy. All the responsibilities of Will's fishing business had fallen to him. He said to tell you that he would write as soon as he had a little free time. Alfie felt terrible about Uncle Will, but she was relieved that Guy still thought of her. She was always afraid he would meet someone while she was gone and get serious about her. Maybe she should go home. Gussie's health was better, and Alfie was homesick. She felt better having made that decision. She would call home later that day.

The day was hectic. The invitations were mailed. After they had gone over the list ten times to make sure no one had been missed. They tried on evening clothes all afternoon. Alfie had an appointment with Gussie's hair dresser in the morning. She wanted a sophisticated look. Her long hair made her look like a child. The party was ten days away and there was so much to do. Alfie stood under the shower, the water seemed to revitalize her. She creamed her body. The cool cotton nightie felt good. She stepped onto the thick cranberry carpet. It looked like velvet. The maid had turned back the covers of her bed. All Alfie wanted to do was sleep. She slipped between the soft pink sheets. She looked at the telephone beside her bed. She wanted to call everybody. She looked at the small gold clock on her night stand. Eleven p.m. Maybe she should wait until tomorrow. She knew that Guy would still be up. Maybe she would call him and wait until morning to call her uncle. She dialed his number. The phone rang four times. Maybe he was asleep. The phone clicked. A voice on the other end said "hello." It was a woman. She must have dialed the wrong number. She apologized, telling the woman she was trying to reach Guy Easterman. The woman said wait a minute, she would get Guy.

A sick feeling stabbed Alfie all over. She couldn't speak. Guy was on the phone. "Hello, this is Guy." "Guy," Alfie managed to compose herself. He recognized her voice. "Hey, Alfie. How are you? Gee, it sure is good to hear your voice." "It's good to hear your voice too. Did I pick a bad time to call?" "Are you kidding. A bad time to call. I can't think of anyone I'd rather hear from than you. Is everything all right?" "Everything's great, but I'm homesick. How's Uncle Will?" "He's doing better. Every day he gets a little stronger. He had a mild stroke. The doctors say he'll live a long time if he retires now. That's why I've been too busy to write. Your uncle told you that, didn't he?" "Yes, in fact I just received the letter today. I thought I'd call since I haven't talked to any of you in such a long time. And I wanted to find out how Uncle Will was doing. I was going to call Uncle Frank, but I knew he would be asleep. He always goes to bed by nine." "Yeah, I went by there on my way home and he was already asleep and that was around eight. He hasn't felt too good lately. I've been checking on him every day. I think he misses you. We all miss you. When are you coming home?"

Alfie's heart raced. She wished she could reach through the phone and touch him. "I'll be home in a month." Alfie had made up her mind at that second when she was going home. "I didn't know Uncle Frank had been sick. He didn't say anything in his letter. If you only knew how much I miss you, all of you." She wanted to ask about the woman who had answered the phone. No, she couldn't do it. "We hired a woman to stay with Uncle Will for a couple of weeks. The doctor thought it would be a good idea. She answered the phone when you called Her name is Jamie, Jamie Jackson. She went to school with your sis. She's a registered nurse, a darned good one, too. I don't know what we'd have done without her." "I'm glad you have someone so reliable. Thanks for looking in on Uncle Frank. But with Aunt Kathy there, I'm not too worried. I hope she hasn't been sick, too. You know it's been almost a year since I left." It felt like ten years. But that would all be in the past soon, very soon. They said their good-byes and Alfie fell into a deep, peaceful sleep.

chapter eleven

THE GALA EVENT

IT LOOKED TO ALFIE as if somebody had just died. There were fresh flowers on every table. Long buffet tables were being set up in the massive dining room. Four fat pigs were cooking in pits under the earth while the cooks barbecued six sides of beef. There was every kind of salad imaginable and baked beans from an old Texas recipe. Chocolate cake, pineapple upside down cake, peach cobbler, apple cobbler, cheesecake and angel food cakes filled the house with a sweet aroma, making Alfie's mouth water at the thought of biting into these delicacies. Hot home made rolls were being cooked in sheet pans. There were thirty kegs of beer and a bar stocked with just about every kind of bourbon, vodka, gin, scotch and sweet liqueur that anyone could name. Lou had even made a trip to his personal wine cellar and a wine rack full of his rare wines stood in the dining room next to a mound of fine crystal wine glasses. Pink china plates with the initials "L. G." were being checked for spots. There were pink crystal water glasses and heavy, dark brown glass beer mugs. Every one of them had the initials "L. G." A band had been hired to play oldies but goodies and anything else anyone would want to hear. Gussie was in rare form. The breast which had been removed hardly crossed her mind. After all, there was a new one in its place. Everyone was tanned, happy and filthy rich. What more could a person ask for?

Alfie too was financially secure. She had never had to worry about money. She felt at ease among these people. When her parents were killed, their insurance settlement had amounted to five hundred thousand dollars. The money had been divided between Alfie and Gussie and put into trust funds until they were of legal age. The court had a certain amount drawn out each year for their living expenses. Uncle Frank didn't want them to do that, said he could take care of the girls himself, but it was a court order and that was that. When Gussie had married Lou, she had her trust fund transferred to Alfie's. Alfie stood before the long mirror in her room admiring her short curly hair. She laughed out loud thinking of Georgio. When Gussie took her into Georgio's, he had taken one look at her waist length hair and placed his hand on his hip while he dangled the other one in the air.

"Oh, my gawd, lovey, you didn't tell me you were bringing in Alice in Wonderland. You should have made her an appointment with the Mad Hatter." He picked up her hair with one hand and let it drop.

Alfie was hysterical with laughter. He opened his eyes wide and puckered his lips. "Well, let's get started. We want to be finished by day after tomorrow. This is going to cost you, lovey." He nodded his head at Gussie and smiled. "The word is out that the party of the year is being given by guess who?" He smiled that little cat-caught-the-canary smile again. "And everybody who's anybody will be there. I do hope my invitation is in the mail, lovey." Georgio, you fix the hair of every woman that's attending that party. Do you think I would have that many women and forget their hairdresser. The invitations were mailed out yesterday." Georgio squealed and grabbed Gussie's face between his hands, planting kisses on her face. And Alfie's hair turned out to be stunning.

Alfie applied her makeup carefully. Just a touch of light smoke eye shadow. She applied the mascara carefully. Her lashes looked long and full. Her green eyes glowed like emeralds. She applied soft peach lipstick to her full lips. A little blush and a few strokes through her hair with the brush. There, now for the finale. Her dress was made of midnight-blue sequins. It was cut straight across the top, plunging to a deep "V" in the back. The dress hugged each curve, a split up the back of the skirt allowed the room for her to walk. Her dark tan looked even darker. Her two-carat diamonds on each ear were a perfect accent. She slipped her midnight-blue satin sandals onto her feet. Her strawberry-blond hair hugged her head in soft curls. She admired the woman that stared back at her from the full length mirror.

Gussie added the finishing touches to her face. She patted her flawless complexion with a little powder. Her long blond hair had been swept up into a perfect Gibson. She slipped the Dior gown over her bottom. The blood red silk gown hung to the floor. The long sleeves came up to the shoulders and the front plunged into a "V". Just enough breast showed. The gown was fitted, shaping Gussie's body into an hourglass. From her knees, the material flowed out, barely brushing the floor. She added a blood red lipstick. The contrast was striking. A maid fastened Gussie's necklace around her slim, graceful neck. The gold chain was so fine it could hardly be seen. At the end of the chain a ten-carat ruby hung right above her cleavage. Ruby earrings hung from her ears. She slid her slim feet into her matching blood- red, silk pumps. A large ruby graced the toe of each shoe.

The sisters came out of their doors at the same time as if it had been planned. They looked at each other and smiled. They stood at the top of the stairs. There was no need to compliment each other. Each knew there would be no others that would come close to their beauty tonight, not even close. Now down to welcome their guests and make this evening one to remember. Lou was dressed in a black western suit. The lapels were studded lightly with black onyx stones. His off white silk shirt had one black onyx stone on each collar tab. A thick, black cord tie was fitted tightly up to his throat with a ten-carat black onyx set in 24 carat gold. His black western boots had the same precious stones. Alfie wished her Uncle

Frank could be here to see this. He would see some of the real "old money" people.

The night was dazzling. The women and men were dressed in their finest. Diamonds, rubies, and emeralds were sparkling on each finger, toe and garment. Alfie was introduced to every big oil man in Texas. She danced with almost every man there. Georgio came dressed in white with the exception of his jade- green shirt and the jade hankie that draped his front top pocket. His jet-black hair, exquisitely styled and his piercing blue eyes made all the guests do a double take. Each of his long, slim, masculine hands was covered with dark green jade rings. The last guest left at four a.m. Tired but happy, Lou put his arms around the girls and the three ascended the winding staircase. There were maids to help them undress and put away their clothes. Their eyes were closed before their heads hit the pillows. And all to soon a month had flown by, Alfie's heart ached at the thought of leaving Gussie but there was a different ache at the thought of seeing Guy.

chapter twelve

PARTING

THE DRIVE TO THE airport was short. A sadness hung in the air. Gussie was dabbing at her eyes under the dark shades she wore. Lou, trying to keep the conversation light and funny, telling several jokes and laughing louder than usual. The skycap hurried to take the luggage - Ronnie Lee. Deja vu. Western Airline passengers now boarding for Los Angeles, San Diego...the voice drowned in the background as the sisters hugged each other and cried. There were promises to visit at least every six months. Alfie hugged Lou, knowing that she would miss this good, kind, extremely generous man. Lou handed Alfie an envelope. "Open it when you get home, not before, you hear now?" He grinned, with the big cigar sticking from his mouth. She knew the envelope contained several shares in his oil empire. She was excited and nervous. Her Uncle was meeting her at the airport. She had missed him and Aunt Kathy so much.

The "no smoking" sign went off. The seat belts had to be kept on because of turbulence over the ocean. The lady next to Alfie was squeezing the arms of the seat so hard her knuckles had turned white. Alfie could never understand why anyone so afraid would fly. She smoothed her dress over her knees. She wore a cream colored, strapless "Lillie Anne" with a matching short-sleeved jacket made of dacron and linen. A simple teardrop diamond hung around her neck. Her tan, a deep bronze, made every woman on the plane envious. A small strap across her toes held the soft cream-colored sandal heels on her feet. She carried a small matching clutch purse. She was not the same Alfie that had left Pink Shell Island one year ago. She was a beautiful young woman. Poised, polished and sure of herself. She laid her head against the seat and closed her eyes.

chapter thirteen

ANXIETIES

GUY KNEW HE WAS early. Her plane wouldn't be in for another half hour. He wondered if she would be surprised to see him here. He sat on a stool in the dark lounge. He ordered a tonic water with lime. Several women who were sitting together started whispering as their eyes drank in Guy's fabulous face and body. His gold- tanned body, sky-blue eyes and his wheat-colored hair with its soft wave made him a candidate for the centerfold of "Playboy." Yet his dark blue slacks and shirt with a powder-blue sports coat and soft dark blue Italian leather shoes gave him the appearance of a very successful business man. He heard the flight attendant announce that Alfie's plane was landing. He felt funny in his stomach.

The passengers hurried through the door. Alfie craned her neck to see where Uncle Will and Aunt Kathy were. Guy was looking for Alfie. Maybe she missed the plane. Their eyes locked. "Wow," thought Guy, where was the little girl he was looking for? Who was this gorgeous creature? This woman with the petite straight nose, full soft lips and oval-shaped face. and huge green eyes laughed at him. He had changed too. He had matured. His face was no longer that of a nice looking boy, but a very handsome man. He had a leaner look, which caused the slight crook in his nose to stand out, just enough for a rugged, manly appearance that demanded respect, giving him a look of confidence. Their first steps toward each other were slow, but together they both broke out in big grins and ran to embrace each other. Then Guy pushed her back, putting his hands around her waist and looked at her for a second. Then again his arms were around her hugging her close to his chest. She was hugging him back. How long had she dreamed of feeling his arms around her like this? Her heart was pounding. She knew he could hear it and didn't care. This was her first glimpse at heaven and he was the man she wanted to share it with.

He said, "You grew up. I'm glad. I thought I would have to wait forever." Her perfume filled his nostrils. Alfie smiled as she said " Oh, don't tell me that. I can't imagine you ever waiting for any girl." Alfie was surprised she could voice those words so easily, yes she had grown. And not just in body.

"Okay, you can think that if it pleases you, but in truth Alfie, you've been special to me since the first time we met." They walked to his car with their arms around each other.

On the way to Uncle Frank's the conversation was filled with all that had been happening to family and each other's lives for the past year. She didn't take her eyes off him. She drank in every inch of his body. His hand squeezed her hand. His touch seemed to burn her skin. She knew he was headed for their favorite spot as he turned the car off the main road. He drove for a few minutes down a narrow sandy road. He stopped the car. She held her breath. She had almost forgotton how beautiful it was.

He held her hand as they slid down a small sandy hill. The huge gray boulders secluded that small stretch of beach. The white sand and pink shells told her she was home. Guy pulled her close. . He slipped her jacket off as he softly kissed her lips, letting his mouth trail down her neck and shoulders, then he gently pulled her close, Her kisses were sweet and innocent He kissed her eyes, her nose, her ears. Their bodies were on fire..

Guy's voice was husky with passion as he said, "I've loved you all my life. I'll never let you walk out of my life again." Tears slid down Alfie's face as he kissed them away. He lowered her to the sand. His mouth kissed her small perfectly formed body. He wanted her so badly his body shook with emotion.

She dug her nails in his back as they both cried. They knew this moment would have to wait.They both knew they had made the right decision as the waves smashed against the rocks and the earth shook and the 'Old Man in the Sea' smiled. These two had been promised to each other from the beginning of time.

Alfie called Lou and Gussie. She invited them to a wedding. Her wedding. They were married by the Justice of the Peace on Alfie's eighteenth birthday. There was certainly something different about this marriage, but just what, it was hard to say. Maybe it was the love that radiated from the bride and groom and touched everyone in the small chapel. All the family and friends felt that maybe some of it had rubbed off on them. They all felt as if they too had just fallen in love.

Uncle Will died in his sleep. Everything he owned was left to Guy and Jerry. Guy had already taken full charge of the fishing boats. Now the house was his and a piece of property Uncle Will had purchased in town. Jerry had been left with four acres of beach front property and a nice bank account. But not any amount of pleading from Guy could convince Jerry to remain on the Island. Uncle Will had dreamed of having his own store which would sell the finest fishing equipment around. Guy would see that his dream was fulfilled. But first he would have to find someone to help with the fishing boats and crew.

Jim Newman, the III, strolled lazily along the wharf. He stopped beside one of the fishing boats. Guy was shouting at a couple of fishermen. "Hey, Terry, I warned you before man, if you want to stay drunk, you can find another job. And that goes for you too, Pat. Now get your things off my boat and stay off." A smile played around Jim's mouth. This was going to be a piece of cake. He walked toward Guy. Guy and Jim were friends from the first day they met. Jim was a hard worker and handled the men well. He was just what Guy had been looking for. In six months or so, Guy could stay home and start construction on the store in town. He and Alfie were happy. What a break to find someone like Jim.

There was one member of the family that wasn't taken with Jim. In fact, Uncle Frank's mood changed whenever Jim came around. The way he looked at Alfie. No man looked at another man's wife like he did, especially your good friend's wife. There was some hidden mystery behind this Jim and he was up to no good. Why couldn't the others see that? Even Kathy was blinded by his smooth talk and his good looks. Uncle Frank expected women to be blind, but what was wrong with Guy's good judgment? Had he cast a spell over all of them?

Guy continued to go out on the boats with Jim until he felt Jim could handle the crew by himself. There was still a lot Jim had to learn about the sea. Jim did not have the love for the sea that Guy did. Jim thought all the talk about the `Old Man in the Sea' was a lot of garbage. Of course, he didn't tell the men that, or Guy. After all, he was starting his life over for the third time and this time he wanted to make it work. He had to make it work. He couldn't leave the Island. Maybe they wouldn't find him and if they did, he could kiss it all goodbye.

chapter fourteen

THE NIGHTMARE

ALFIE STOOD ON THE wharf watching the old fishing boat slowly pull away from the dock. She read the name on the back of the boat. Jonah. One of the oldest but best built fishing boats that Guy had. She waved to Guy and Jim. She remembered the picture and looked in her sweater pocket, it was gone. She looked up at the boat. Guy had the picture, waving it in his hand. She blew him a kiss. She had wanted to keep the picture. Oh well, she would have it when he returned in a couple of days. This would be his last trip out. How lucky she was. She wanted to pinch herself to make sure she wasn't dreaming. She was more in love with him now than she was the day she married him.

Her legs still felt a little weak from their lovemaking earlier. She could feel his hard lean body pressing her so close she could barely breathe, his hands setting her body on fire. There was an urgency as he pulled her clothes off. He slipped his off just as quickly. She moaned as they slid down to the cool patio floor They were so right for each other. She felt their bodies blend into one. She could never be this good with anyone else, never. They soaped each other in the shower. He dried her. She clung to him. His body felt cool. "Don't go, please don't go. Stay here with me. Can't Jim handle things by himself?" "Hey, this is my last trip out. You know that. I won't ever have to leave you again, not ever. You'll get tired of me being around all the time." She walked back toward the house. She decided to go to Uncle Frank's. Aunt Kathy had been ill with a bad virus that hung on. Uncle Frank always knew how to cheer her up.

Aunt Kathy was cooking, she felt better. They were both happy to see her. Uncle Frank knew Alfie was worried. "Let's take a walk on the pier. I haven't been down there in a while. Always helps me to think. Wanna come, Kathy?" Aunt Kathy begged off. "Let me cook and get a few things done. You two do the walking." "How long is he gonna be gone this time? Is this his last trip?" Uncle Frank stopped walking to light his old pipe, cupping his hand around the match to keep it from going out. Alfie stopped walking and gazed at the ocean. "I'm just being silly. I don't know why I'm worried. This time it's two days. And it's his last. He says Jim will be ready after this."

"I hope Jim works out for him. I know Guy puts a lot of trust in him. You would think in six months you would know a person. He's almost lived at your house. I never liked that. But I have no business putting my two cents in, do I? Maybe my feelings about him are wrong. I hope so. You know I've never cared for him. There's something he's hiding. He looks at you in the wrong way. He's in love with you. I could see that months ago." You're such a wise man." Alfie put her arm through his and laid her head on his shoulder. "I love you. But I think you may be wrong about Jim. He's never made a pass at me. I think he loves me like a sister. If he's hiding something, so what. A lot of people hide things in their past. It doesn't make them all bad. Does it?" Uncle Frank frowned as he said "I hope you're right. Maybe he will be good for Guy. Have you seen Old Sarge around lately?" He was trying to change the touchy subject. Time would tell all.

"Let's talk to the 'Old Man in the Sea.' I haven't talked to him in a long time." Alfie steered her uncle to a huge flat gray rock. The ocean looked rough. The waves were smacking the rocks with great force. The 'Old Man in the Sea' must be angry tonight. Uncle Frank thought he would ask him. "Old Majestic One, are you angry? Your waves beat the rocks and the shore with such great force. Your beautiful sea is a tranquilizer for the people on this little Island. There must be someone here that is not a desirable person."

Alfie knew her uncle was referring to Jim as the undesirable person. Uncle Frank listened to the sounds of the ocean as if he could understand what they were saying. Alfie used to love doing this when she was younger, now some of the excitement was gone. Maybe she was too old to believe in the 'Old

Man in the Sea.' Had she grown up too much to enjoy a little fantasy in her life? Or maybe what Uncle Frank has asked the `Old Man in the Sea' made her feel uneasy.

The next day started out like any other. Except for the anxious feeling in her chest. What was wrong with her? She walked down toward the pier,.down to the edge of the shore. She walked closer, letting the waves cover her feet and ankles. The water was cold. She sat on a rock, digging her toes in the sand. The sky had turned dark. The waves were pounding harder. She loved the ocean. She wanted her ashes spread over the ocean when she died. Her parents were someplace in the sea and she felt she too belonged to these vast waters.

Alfie felt a tear run down her face. `Old Man in the Sea,' I do believe in you. And something is wrong. I feel it. What is it? `Old Wise One,' you know. She fell asleep as she waited for Guy to come home. But Guy didn't come home, only Jim came home. Alfie could hear her uncle telling her that there had been an accident. His lips were moving. It sounded like gibberish. She couldn't understand what it had to do with her. She wanted to know where Guy was. She beat her hands against her Uncles chest. The screams she heard seemed so far away. She wanted to die, she prayed. "Please God let me die."

chapter fifteen

A LIVING HELL

THE NEXT FEW DAYS was a nightmare for Alfie. When would she wake up and find she was dreaming? When would the pain go away? Jerry was there. This was the third time he had been home since he had left the Island. He had come for Uncle Will's funeral, Alfie and Guy's wedding and now for this horrible nightmare.

The pain and grief Jerry felt was etched into his face. How could he comfort Alfie when he felt like someone was inside him tearing his heart out? He and Guy had been through so much together. He could still see Guy crying in the orphanage because he was hungry. Dear God, how can I live through this? How?" He beat his fist against the rocks where he had knelt to pray. The waves splashed over his shoes as the tide came in. He continued to kneel and pray out loud in hopes that it would somehow ease the pain. A calmness came over him. He knew the worst was yet ahead. He would comfort Alfie and do whatever else had to be done. He walked back to the house.

Jerry gave the eulogy. He felt that it was his duty. No one had known Guy better or had loved him more. Jerry had aged before Alfie's eyes. He was a confirmed bachelor. A big man on the Alaskan pipe lines, wealthy, ambitious and handsome. Now he stood humble before the small crowd as he spoke, his voice shaking with emotion. Gussie held Alfie's hand. She saw the color drain from her face as Jerry spoke Guy's name. She stood up to walk from the small church. Her legs felt like silly putty. The world had no color. She opened her eyes. Lou and Gussie were staring down at her. "You okay?" Lou said. "You come home with me and your sis for a few days. It might help to get away. Think about it." Gussie sat on the edge of the bed and gathered Alfie in her arms.

"I've got to go for a walk. I'm okay. Just be here when I get back." Alfie washed her face in the bathroom. She sipped the hot tea Gussie had made for her. "You want me to go with you?" Jerry stood in the living room as Alfie pulled on her sweater. "No. I need to be alone for a little while. I won't be long." She hugged him. Uncle Frank opened the door. She gave him a quick hug, and was afraid that she would start crying again. Where were all the tears coming from? She walked along the beach. The cool breeze felt good. She couldn't believe Guy was dead. She would never believe it. She sat watching the giant waves. Two children ran past laughing, with their parents close behind. Guy would have been a wonderful father. She knew at that moment she would never have another man's child. Gussie stayed for two weeks. Jerry for three. Alfie couldn't wait until she was alone. Jerry made sure all of Alfie's affairs were in order. She would build the store in town. Jim would continue to manage the fishing boats and men for her.

"You will call me if you need anything, won't you?" Jerry was like a mother hen. He wanted to go home and yet he felt obligated to stay with Alfie. "Go home, Jerry. I don't need you here. You have your life and I don't' expect you to give it up for me. I'm a big girl now. I love you for the way you are. But if I get in a mess or need your professional advice for anything, I'll call you. I promise. Now, pack." Jerry hugged Alfie close. "I know why Guy loved you so much. If I could find a girl like you, I might consider getting married, maybe even have a kid or two." The tears poured freely down both their faces. Alfie knew she would miss him.

chapter sixteen

THE HEALING

ALFIE WORKED FIENDISHLY IN the days ahead. She hired a construction crew to build the store. She saw that every detail in Guy's blueprints was followed. Jim managed the fishing boats and crew without any problems. He also managed to find time to help Alfie with the construction crew, making sure all went according to plan. He was around the house a lot fixing little things that Alfie knew nothing about. Uncle Frank was ready to admit he had been wrong about Jim. Jim made no advances toward Alfie. Alfie had no time for any of her friends. She had completely isolated herself from almost everyone but her family and Jim, and her best friend Cassie who lived next door. The store was completed. It was beautiful. Only the latest and finest equipment was stocked. Alfie said to herself, "Okay, Uncle Will. This was your dream. Guy wanted to make it come true and it has." She felt proud. Proud and empty.

chapter seventeen

THE STROKING

JIM FEELINGS FOR ALFIE deepened in the weeks ahead. He had never been in love so to Jim it must be lust, oh well time would tell.. She started to depend on him, asking his advice before she would make a final decision on anything. The store in town was thriving. Jim helped Alfie interview a hundred people before she decided that Cole Marshall was to run the store. He had lived all of his 52 years on Pink Shell Island. He knew everyone in town and the ones he didn't know, were strangers to him only as long as it took him to ask their names and find out where they were from. He took charge of ordering all fishing equipment and helped with the bookwork. He was certainly worth more than the salary he had requested. Alfie had just increased his pay. She wanted to see Cole's face when he opened his pay envelope. Cole Marshall thought the world of Alfie. He had worked for her Uncle Frank for a spell. Good people. A shame that nice husband of hers had to drown. As for Jim, well he didn't care for him at all. Nope. There was something about Jim that he just couldn't put his finger on. He was sneaky, downright sneaky. But he couldn't say that to Alfie. She thought Jim was great. And maybe he was, for her. And maybe he was just using her.

Jim finished tightening the pipe under the sink. That should hold it, he thought. He gathered his tools off the floor and placed them in his tool bag. He looked around for Alfie. Maybe she was in the basement. He started up the hall. He wanted to use the bathroom and wash up before he headed for the wharf. Alfie was standing in front of the full length mirror, rubbing oil on her body. A towel lay at her feet .Her body, a golden brown was firm and young. Her wet strawberry blond hair hugged her head in soft curls. She thought of Guy and felt the stabbing pain in her chest return. She missed him so much, she hated the thought of living without him. A lump had already started to form in her throat. Jim passed the bedroom door, he stopped. His eyes rested on Alfie's perfectly formed body that glistened from a ray of sun, from a small window. He ached all over, he wanted her so badly he could hardly gain control of himself. He wanted to turn and walk away before Alfie noticed him standing there, but his feet felt glued to the floor. His eyes met Alfie's as she gasped and her hands grabbed the towel around her feet covering the front of her as she ran and slammed the bedroom door. She lay her body against the cool wood, her face burning with embarrassment. She felt cheapened. It was as though Jim had intruded on her most private thoughts. Jim knew there was no use trying to talk to Alfie. He had seen the look in her eyes. Now, it would take a lot of hard work to gain her trust again.

Alfie prepared the ribs for dinner, Uncle Frank, Aunt Kathy, Uncle Will and Old Sarge would be here in less than an hour. She was still shaken from the incident with Jim this morning. Yet, she knew they would have to talk. He was also coming for dinner. She would have to be calm, there had to be an explanation. To say she would never see him again, well that was totally absurd. After all, he did handle the majority of her business affairs. And wasn't he always around when she needed him. Repairing whatever needed to be repaired in the house. Why he even had his own key. Jim was the first to arrive. Alfie let him in. Avoiding his eyes she said, "The others should be here any minute, make yourself a drink while I finish setting the table." Alfie turned to walk away. Alfie felt Jim's hand on her arm. She gasped as he gently turned her to face him. She could see the pained expression on his face. He said "I'm sorry, Alfie, can you forgive me?" He sounded so sincere. Alfie nodded yes as she lowered her head. Jim's hand slid off her arm as Alfie turned to walk away. She stopped, and with her back still to Jim she said, "It was my fault too. I should have closed the bedroom door, I'm just so used to being by myself in the house." Her words trailed off as a lump formed in her throat. Yes, she was always by herself. The pain of loneliness stabbed in her heart once again.

Her mind came back to the present. She lifted herself off of the lounge chair and grabbed for a glass that almost fell over. She walked into the cool kitchen and filled her glass with ice cubes. It had been a year since she and Jim had been married. The fishing business and the store in town were in good shape financially. But Alfie was not all right. She could feel someone watching her all the time. And yet there was no one. Sometimes she thought she was going mad. Maybe she was having a nervous breakdown. There was a logical explanation. There had to be. She would tell Jim how she felt. He would know what to do. But then he would worry. She didn't want that. And the dreams. What about the dreams? She could tell Cassie. Cassie, her best friend, would listen to her.

chapter eighteen

CASSIE

JUST GETTING THE CHILDREN off to school had exhausted Cassie. She let her body drop to the sofa. The words of Dr. Jordan ran back through her mind. "Cassie, we have the results of your test." He sat sideways on the edge of the desk, one foot on the floor. He had her folder open in his slender, well scrubbed hands. They looked pink, tender, professional. Cassie waited. Her own hands, twisting the strap of her blue purse. She looked down at her lap. She pulled the pale blue linen dress tighter over her small knees. Cassie was a petite size five with small, sharp features, big dark brown eyes and short, dark, curly hair. Too curly, in fact... almost kinky. Sweat trickled down her face from the edge of her hair. Why didn't he say something? She wanted to scream. She found her voice, "What were the results?"

Dr. Jordan looked up from her folder, his face blank as if he were wondering why she was here. Then a look of recognition came into his eyes. "Cassie, you have Sickle Cell Anemia. As of right now, there is no known cure. But with modern medicine, we could have one tomorrow. You didn't tell me you were Negro, or part Negro. Was it your mother, your father?" He didn't wait for her to answer. Cassie's body grew hot. Her face was burning. She was twisting the strap of her purse so tightly that her fingers were white. "White, White, White. I'm White," she wanted to scream.

"Only the black race have Sickle Cell Anemia. Why, we don't know. You'll have to be hospitalized every so often. She saw his lips moving. He was writing out a prescription. He handed it to her. "For pain. You'll need it." He closed the folder. "Please make an appointment with the nurse. I want to see you in two weeks." He looked down at her, reached out and squeezed her hand. He said, "I'm sorry." She paid the receptionist, and put the appointment card in her purse. She felt numb.

She slid behind the wheel of her Toyota. She laid her head on the steering wheel. Black, Black. Only Blacks have Sickle Cell Anemia. She moaned out loud. "Oh, dear God, no." Her head was pounding. How could she tell Jay that she was part Negro? When her parents had adopted her, she had been two months old. They hadn't cared that she was part Negro. Her features were White. They had waited such a long time to have a baby girl, and they loved her as if she were their very own. She was raised White. She thought

White and she looked White. She remembered the day her parents decided to tell her that she had been adopted and that her father had been a Negro.

Her father took her arm and guided her to the sofa. "Sit down, Cassie. I have to talk to you. One day you'll get married and have babies. When you have a baby, your baby could be dark. You see, Cassie, we couldn't have babies so we adopted you." Cassie looked at him with a puzzled expression on her face. "What do you mean, dark, Daddy?" Cassie, at eighteen, was very naive. Her father took her hands in his. Tears welled up in his eyes. "We wanted a baby so badly. When we saw you we fell in love with you right away. You were so beautiful. When the agency told us you had a Negro father, we didn't care. Color means nothing to us, Cassie. It doesn't matter what color a man is, but what's in his heart that makes the man." He blew his nose.

How many times had she heard her father say that? All her life he had been conditioning her for this moment. Her heart was pounding. Her world started to crumble. She fell, sobbing, into her father's arms. She loved her parents. They had given her everything. Her parents stood in the doorway of her bedroom as she packed her suitcase. They understood. She would stay with her father's sister, Aunt Suzie, in Southern California. Aunt Suzie needed someone to live with her. She was seventy-six and alone. With her money she could hire someone, but Aunt Suzie was cheap. She knew that by having Cassie stay with her, she would save money.

Cassie clung to her parents. They were all crying. Her mother said, "We love you so much, baby. Don't hate us." Cassie stopped crying. She looked at her parents. "I could never hate you, Mama." She looked at her father. "Just tell me one thing, Daddy. Am I White or am I Black. What color am I?" Her father blew his nose. "Why do you have to be a color? Just be you."

Cassie fell in love with Pink Shell Island and with Jay Carusso. When they were married, Cassie told him nothing of her past. There seemed to be no need to. She would never have children. It was as simple as that. In less than a year she was pregnant. She looked at the doctor. "There must be some mistake. I'm on birth control pills." She lived in fear as the child grew inside her. What would she do if the baby were black? Her labor was long and difficult, finally ending in a Caesarian Section. She opened her eyes. Jay was standing by her bed, along with her father and mother. A worried look was on their faces. Her parents knew she had told Jay nothing of her past. Their expressions changed as they saw her eyes open. Their frowns changed to smiles. Her father said, "You have a beautiful little girl. Just like you when you were a baby." He winked.

Thank God, Cassie thought. She lived through the same fear with her second child. Another C-Section. The doctor feared for her life this time, and performed a tubal ligation. Jay, Jr. was whiter than her little girl, Ginny. Cassie's secret was safe. Until now. She turned the key in the ignition. She looked to the side before pulling out. The sun was starting to set. The pink and blue sky looked like a painting. She knew she would never tell Jay. He would hate her. She would tell Alfie, her closest friend. But would she still be her friend when she knew?

Well, time would tell.

Alfie knocked harder. She knew Cassie was home. The children had just left for school. Cassie opened the door. She smiled. "Hi, come on in. I was in the back bedroom. Have you been knocking long?" She stepped aside to let Alfie in. "Not long," Alfie said. "Where's the coffee? I'm dying for a cup. I've decided I'm not even going to try and make anymore." She hugged Cassie. "Are you all right? You look a little pale." Cassie poured coffee into two gray mugs. "I must have a touch of the stomach flu. Nothing serious. I'm okay. I think I'll just lay around today and take it easy." They sat down at the table. Cassie looked at Alfie. She could tell that something was wrong.

"And what are you worried about? Come on. Tell me." Cassie was thankful for any diversion from her problem. Alfie added cream and two spoons of sugar to her coffee. "I think I'm losing my mind." She looked at the smile that played around Cassie's mouth. "Cassie, I'm not joking. I feel like I'm being watched everywhere I go, even in my own house. What's wrong with me?" Cassie knew that Alfie was serious. "How long have you felt this way? Have you told Jim?" Alfie shook her head, no, as she reached for a Tissue to catch the tears that were making their way down her cheeks. Cassie reached for Alfie's hand. "Don't cry, honey. Maybe someone is watching you. Why not call Jesse and report it."

Alfie laughed, blowing her nose into a fresh tissue. "Oh, Cassie. I love you. Jesse would really think I'm a kook. What would I report? I haven't seen anyone. I just feel like I'm being watched. Maybe I need to see a shrink." "Maybe you've been working too hard. Get away for a few weeks. Go see your sis. If you're worried about leaving Jim, don't. He can eat his meals with us. Jay would love that and I don't mind." "I know you don't, Cassie. That's another thing that's wrong. I'm not worried about Jim. I never worry about him. He would have been better off if he hadn't married me." She wiped away fresh tears. "When I make love to Jim, I think of Guy. I dream of Guy. In my dreams, he's alive. He's hurt and he needs me. The dreams are so real." She blew her nose again. "I dream that I'm looking for Guy. I can hear him calling my name. The `Old Man in the Sea' picks me up in his hand. All of a sudden, I'm in a bubble, a big pink bubble. I can't see out because of the pink color. I beat against the sides. It feels like soft rubber. I'm floating and Guy's voice is getting closer, so I beat the sides of the bubble harder. The `Old Man' holds his hand up and says, `Stop, wait, and soon you will see him.' I don't understand why I dream that same dream over and over."

"Oh, Cassie, I don't think Guy's dead. Do you think I'm crazy to feel that way?" "You know I don't think you're crazy. I don't know what to think about your dreams. Maybe Dr. Chetnie could tell you why you dream the same dream over and over. And as far as Guy's being dead, if he's not dead, where is he?" Cassie decided to wait until later to tell Alfie her problem. Cassie took her medicine. The pain in her stomach went away.

Alfie pulled on her bikini. The sun felt great. She felt better already. Having a friend to confide in was the best therapy yet.

chapter nineteen

DOMINIC, THE PAST

THE EVENING WAS COOL. Jim was quiet as he barbecued steaks on the patio. The sound of the surf was soothing. The tension ebbed slowly from his body. He thought of how different his life was now compared to over a year ago. But then you couldn't call the way he had lived before he came to Pink Shell Island really living. And Alfie, well, there was no one like her. But then, the women he used to know could hardly be compared to Alfie. Alfie was his life. It wasn't love but it was as near to it as he could feel, anyway. When Guy introduced them, he knew he had to have her regardless of the fact that she already had a husband. Now she was his and in time she would love him, and maybe he would learn to love her. It would only take time, and he had plenty of that.

Alfie walked onto the patio. She handed Jim a Beefeaters on the rocks. She took a sip of her brandy.

A warm feeling spread through her body. She leaned over and kissed Jim on the cheek. He grabbed her arm. "Hey, you can do better than that." He pulled her close, covering her mouth with his. She returned the kiss. She pulled away. "You'll burn the steaks." He remembered how she had responded to Guy when he touched her. She melted at Guy's touch. Just the thought of Guy wracked his body with jealousy. How could he be jealous of a dead man? But he was. He made himself calm down. She was his and Guy was dead, so why worry about the past. He would wipe Guy from his mind just as he had wiped his would be Mother from it, just thinking of her made him want to kill her.Burning in the fire had been to good for her.

He remembered the rat-infested flat in New York. The cold beans from old dented cans with no labels. The bed he shared with his three little brothers, and the stinking sheets which were never washed. His baby brother cried constantly. Jim had walked the floor with him many nights until the baby finally slept from exhaustion. He remembered the night little Timmy wouldn't stop crying. His face was red. He was sick and burning with fever. Dominic was scared. His mother had come home with a new man. There was a new one almost every night. They were both drunk. He rinsed Timmy's bottle out in the rusty roach infested sink. The milk in the bottle had been clabbered. He filled the bottle with cold water. He went to his mother's bedroom door and pushed the door open. "Mom, Mom. Timmy's sick, Mom. He feels real hot. He's really sick, Mom." The room was dark. He heard low moans and the mattress was creaking.

Dominic's heart was pounding. He walked closer to the bed. He felt fear knot his stomach, but he couldn't let his brother die. He reached out to feel for his mother. His hand touched someone. "Mom, Timmy's real sick, Mom. He's hot as fire." A big hand shot out catching him on the side of the head. He saw stars. Timmy fell from his arms. Timmy's cries turned into screams as he hit the floor. Dominic picked himself up, grabbed Timmy and ran from the apartment. Timmy's screams could be heard throughout the building. Dominic ran into the street carrying six months old Timmy. He was crying. He thought of his two brothers still upstairs in bed. Joel was two years old and Sammy was three. A police patrol car stopped beside Dominic who was crying and shaking so hard that he could hardly speak. The police officers were not the ones who usually patrolled this area. These two were older and looked sympathetic as they placed Dominic and Timmy in the patrol car. Dominic and the officers waited in County General Hospital as the doctor examined Timmy.

A small, frail looking doctor with a slight hump in his back came through the swinging doors marked "Emergency." He barely took his eyes from the folder in his hands as he acknowledged the officers with a nod of his head. "The boy's in bad shape. Double pneumonia. Severe anemia. Looks like a case of child neglect. The parents should be locked up. Such a shame." The doctor shook his head. He looked at Sergeant Nelson. "Can I talk to you a minute?"

The patrol car moved through the darkened streets. The sergeant had made arrangements with the Welfare Department to meet one of the social workers at Dominic's apartment building. They would take Dominic and his other two brothers to Child Haven, a receiving home for neglected and orphaned children. The sergeant's eyes filled with tears as he looked at the small, dirty boy through the rear-view mirror of the patrol car. It would break the boy's heart if he knew little Timmy wouldn't make it through the night.

Sergeant Nelson thought of his own happy childhood. He remembered the way his mother's laughter would ring in his ears as she lifted him up and planted kisses all over his face . The smell of freshly baked fruitcakes and sugar cookies had filled the air. Then he would be handed to his father who would swing him high, then hug him close. He had loved the way his father always smelled of Old Spice. They had always treated him like a precious jewel. Dominic would never know a happy childhood. Dominic fought back tears as he looked out of the patrol car window. The car turned onto his street. Red lights flashed in the distance. The red lights donned the top of four long fire trucks that sat in front of the building where Dominic lived. Huge streams of water pushed at the fire that leaped from the windows of the old building. Human balls of fire jumped from the towering inferno. Dominic would hear their screams for the rest of his life. There were no door handles on the doors of the patrol car. Dominic screamed and beat at the door.

Officer Nelson opened the door catching Dominic in his arms as he tried to rush past. "Let me go," Dominic screamed. "I've got to save my brothers. Please, somebody, help them." Dominic's struggles to get loose stopped as he heard one of the firemen say, "No one could live through that. These old buildings should have been condemned years ago. They're all fire traps." Dominic watched as charred bodies were removed. They were burned beyond recognition. He was taken alone to Child Haven. He cried for little Sammy and Joel. He cried when Officer Nelson told him that Timmy had died, and Officer Nelson had cried with him. Dominic never cried for his mother. In fact, he vowed never to think of her again. Hate was strong in the heart of Dominic Paveritti. He ran away from Child Haven so many times that soon they no longer bothered to look for him. He lived with the hobos and rode the freights. He grew quickly and his heart grew hard with each passing day.

At the age of seventeen he had taken to the streets. Ruthless and unfeeling, he had made a name for himself. No one would challenge him. He used people to get what he wanted. Especially women. And with his good looks there was never a lack of those. His reputation soon attracted the Mafia. He was just the kind of person that they were looking for. He made his way to the top list of their hit men. Even killing people didn't phase Dominic. He would think of his mother and kill her over and over and over again. He was always on the move. He wore the finest clothes and his manicured hands were heavy with diamonds. He drove the latest Mazaretti. He was soon the biggest hit man in New York. He was one of the Mafia's most valuable men. At thirty years of age, he was a millionaire, but still something was missing in his life. He knew that it was time for a change. One more big job and he was leaving the Big Apple. He had already made the arrangements, knowing that the mob would never let him go. Dominic stood over the body of the governor. He reached down and removed his wallet. The drawers of the governor's desk lay on the floor. Papers were everywhere. A simple case of burglary. He knew the police would know it was his work, but there was no way they could prove it. They had been trying to put him behind bars for thirteen years.

He unbuckled the holster strap from around his chest. He lay his Smith and Wesson on the nightstand. Grabbing his suitcase from the closet, he began to pack. He looked around the room, making sure that he had left nothing. He showered and slipped on a pair of western jeans and a plaid shirt. He shoved his feet into the new, soft, dark-red leather boots. He buckled the shoulder holster into place. He checked the gun, making sure the safety was on. He slipped on a light weight western cut sports jacket. He lit a fat Tampa cigar, and stuck it in the side of his mouth. He opened the door and swung the valise over his shoulder as he lifted the suitcase with his other hand. He left the door open. The smell of his Paco Raban lingered in the hotel room long after he had left. There were a couple of things he must take care of before he left the Big Apple.

He stopped at the desk and handed the desk clerk a long manila envelope. He said, "A man by the name of Nelson will be by to pick this up in a day or two." The desk clerk started to protest until Dominic shoved a hundred dollar bill under his nose. The clerk said, "Yes, sir. No problem, sir." A bell man was at Dominic's side, lifting his luggage. "Your car, sir?" "No, get me a taxi." Dominic pressed twenty dollars into the bell man's coat pocket.The envelope he left with the desk clerk contained the pink slip and the keys to the Mazaretti. Every pair of eyes in the hotel lobby stared at this tall slim handsome man. His black curly hair and Grecian nose gave him a rugged look. His olive complexion and aqua blue eyes melted every woman who saw him. He glanced at his Swiss-made Patek Phillipe watch. Four hours before he had to be at the dock. He would have to hurry.

The cab circled the narrow, winding streets of the cemetery. Dominic held up his hand. "Stop. And wait." The cabby pulled to the curb and stopped. Dominic walked over to the three graves. He looked at the new headstones and was satisfied. The small graves had fresh flowers. He had paid the caretaker well. He was glad that he had moved the boys from the small, un-kept cemetery in which the County had buried them. He remembered the small, timid-looking man whom he had dealt with. He had asked Dominic, "You want your mother moved along with your brothers, don't you?" Dominic spat on the ground, barely missing the man's shoe. Grabbing the front of the man's shirt and pulling him close to his face so that their eyes met, he said, "They never had a mother." The little man saw cold, unfeeling eyes filled with a hate such as he had never seen in his life. His old body shivered for hours after Dominic Paveritti had left. Dominic knelt by the graves. He took out a pocket knife and dug a hole about five inches deep next to each headstone. He peeled off three one hundred dollar bills. He stuck one in each hole. He smoothed the dirt, placing the small patch of grass back that he had so carefully cut out. Pictures of these small boys clicked in his mind like a camera. A lump formed in Dominic's throat as he heard the screams of Timmy in his mind and smelled the clabbered milk in the dirty bottle. He heard the hungry cries of Joel and Sammy and smelled the rank pee on the dingy sheets.

Dominic stood and walked away from the graves for the last time.

The cab pulled to the front of the train station. Dominic bought a newspaper, pressing a fifty dollar bill in the blind man's hand. He stood in the stall of the toilet and slipped off his coat, unstrapping his shoulder holster. He wrapped the newspaper around the gun and holster. He slipped on his sports jacket and pulled a key from his pocket. He slipped the newspaper into the locker and made sure that the door was securely closed. Turning, he walked back into the men's room. He pulled toilet paper from the roll and wrapped it around the small key. He threw the toilet paper into the toilet and flushed. He flushed again and again. The seat of the cab was hot as he laid his head back. One more stop. He closed his eyes. His head was pounding. The cab stopped in front of the Halfway House, a bar that sat on the corner of East 25th and Lexington, two blocks from the 23rd Police Precinct. Dominic told the cabby to wait. He squinted as his eyes became adjusted to the darkness of the bar. He dropped a dime into the pay phone and dialed the number for the 23rd Precinct. "Twenty-third Precinct. Sergeant Waller here." Dominic said, "Yes, Sergeant Nelson's office, please." Sergeant Nelson's phone rang three times. Dominic was ready to hang up when he heard the Sergeant's familiar voice. "Sergeant Nelson speaking." "Nelson, it's Paveritti." There was a moment of silence. The Sergeant answered in a low voice, "Where are you?" "The usual place. I need to see you right away." Dominic hung up the phone and made his way to a booth in the far corner of the bar. He lit a Tampa.

Bouncing as he walked, a tall black man dressed in a gray sharkskin suit with layers of gold draped around his neck, approached the booth. The black man grinned, his white teeth the only things visible in the dark corner. He held out his hands palms up for their usual greeting. Dominic met them with his. The black man said in a low voice, "Hey, blood. If it ain't my main man. What it is, brother, what it is?" He turned and signaled for the cocktail waitress. She walked to the bar and ordered Beefeaters on the rocks. She knew who was in the back booth. No one else sat there. Curtis slid into the other side of the booth. The cocktail waitress sat the gin in front of Dominic and a Perrier in front of Curtis. Dominic took a long drink. Curtis had a worried look on his face as he said, "Your name is on the lips of everyone brother,.I thought you would be halfway to Mars by now, not here at the Halfway House. Man, you ain't safe nowhere. Everyone knows nobody could have hit the big man but you and got away without a trace. Brother, you got to get out of town." There was a knock on the back door next to their booth. Dominic looked at Curtis and said, "I'm leaving for Mars today Curtis, but there were a few things I had to do and a few friends I had to see before I left. That's Nelson at the back door now. Will you let him in?"

Curtis let Nelson in. Nelson slid into the booth and clasped Dominic's hand. "You're hotter than a firecracker. I thought you would have had the sense to leave by now. What the hell's wrong with you?" "I'm leaving now. The cab's waiting. But I had to give you this." He handed Nelson a sealed, long white envelope. Dominic said, "There's a large manila envelope at the Hotel Concord. I left it with the desk clerk. It has your name on it. Pick it up." Sergeant Nelson said, "What is it? What is this?" Dominic stood. So did Nelson. Nelson embraced the tall man. It was difficult to blame Dominic for turning to a life of crime. Nelson would always see him as the dirty little boy with a screaming baby in his arms. He could still feel the thin body fighting to free himself while Nelson held him tight and watched his brothers burn to death. He would forever hear the heart breaking cry that tore from Dominic's throat. He had tried to adopt Dominic. All of his efforts had been useless. The Welfare Office believed that Dominic needed both a father and a mother. A father alone would not be adequate. That was the Welfare's argument...Dominic remained alone. Tears slid down Nelson's face. He would never see Dominic Paveritti as a gangster, a hardened criminal, as the biggest hit man in New York. He had scooped Dominic from the hands of the law many times. And he would continue to help him, right or wrong. Dominic loved this old man, in as much as he was capable of feeling any love at all. Dominic pushed gently away. He felt the same lump in his throat he had noticed at the cemetery. Dominic said, "Open it when you get home, okay?" Dominic waited for Nelson to answer. Nelson nodded his head yes, and walked out the back door. He didn't know that he was walking out wealthier by two hundred thousand dollars. Dominic pressed ten big ones into Curtis' hand.

The cab stopped at the dock. It was time to board the giant ocean liner. His new I.D. read Jim Newman, III. The tall buildings blended into the background as Dominic gazed upon the Statue of Liberty for the last time.

chapter twenty

THE PRESENT

THE STEAKS WERE DONE. He would make the evening perfect. He could do anything he set his mind to do. Didn't his being here prove that? Later, in bed, Alfie's passion soared. Jim could make her body beg for more and all she had to do was pretend he was Guy. Afterwards she lay still in his arms. The guilty feelings were still there. How could she rid her mind of them? She wondered even now if Guy had known that Jim had come close to taking advantage of her. Jim had been like one of the family. He was always at their house. And she had loved the extra attention which he had given her. She remembered her uncle's warning and she had laughed. The thought of Jim's being in love with her was ridiculous, but she began to watch him more closely after that. There was a hunger in his eyes which she had never noticed before. She kept her distance. Then it happened. She opened the patio door. The cool house felt good. Her skin was hot from the sun. She untied her bikini top and let it fall to the floor. She removed the bottoms, then started down the hallway to her bedroom. A cool shower would feel good. Jim was coming out of the bedroom. Guy's attache case was in his hand. Alfie had frozen ready to scream, Jim stopped. "Alfie, I didn't think you were home. Guy forgot his attache case and payroll." His words trailed off as he took in her beauty. He sat the attache case on the floor, she didn't move. He reached out to touch her as she screamed and ran into the bedroom, slamming the door and locking it.

She stayed in bed the next two days faking the flu. She was so ashamed. How could she face Jim? But not confiding in Guy had made her feel even guiltier. She knew that Jim wasn't asleep. Was he thinking about Guy? She had to hear him tell her again. One more time. "Tell me again, Jim. Tell me how it happened." Jim's relaxed body stiffened. He took a deep breath. He kissed the top of her head. "We had the fishing nets in the water when the sky turned black and the ocean became a raging nightmare. There was no warning. It happened so fast. The huge wave whipped the old fishing boat, ripping the giant nets from the bow. We all grabbed whatever was near and hung on for our lives. Guy and I were next to each other. The old ship was on its side several times. I saw Guy slide across the deck. He grabbed onto some rope tied to the stern and, another wave washed over the boat. That was the last time I saw Guy. The storm stopped as quickly as it had started." Jim paused and lit a cigarette, inhaling deeply. He continued. "Guy was the only one missing. There was nothing we could do then, and there's nothing we can do now. So why do you want to torture yourself? Does it help to hear it over and over?" He waited for an answer. He heard her even breathing. He mashed his cigarette into the ashtray, then slid down beneath the covers. He knew he would sleep like a baby, nagging conscience or not. He had killed people without blinking an eye. Why was this different? He knew why. He had really liked Guy, oh well. The choices we had to make. Jim remembered the shocked expression on Guy's face as he had pried Guy's hands loose from his arm and Guy had slid to his death.

chapter twenty one

THE FEAR

ALFIE'S EYES RESTED ON the clock. Eight a.m. Jim had left earlier than usual. A note lay next to the clock. "Jim Newman, III, requests the pleasure of your company for cocktails, dinner and dancing. Six o'clock sharp. Be ready, Jim." She felt lazy. She stretched and reaching for the phone, dialed Gussie's number. Gussie's maid answered. "This is the Phillips' residence." "Hello. This is Alfie. Is Gussie there?" "Yes, Ms. Alfie. Just one moment and I'll get her." Gussie's sounded out of breath, "Hello." Hi, were you running? Alfie laughed. "No, I wasn't running. I was walking fast. I was just getting ready to phone you. Must be telepathy. Are you okay?" "Yeah," Alfie said. I'm okay. I just miss you. Come down for a week or two. Both of you." "Lou and I were just talking about it. We're planning to come in a couple of weeks." Gussie squealed. "Oh, Alfie. I wasn't going to tell you until we got there, but I can't wait. I'm pregnant. Can you believe it? After we tried so hard. Then we stopped trying and now I'm pregnant. Lou's so happy you would think he had struck a dozen oil wells." "Oh, my God. I'm going to be an aunt. I'm so happy for you. What did the doctor say? Are you all right? I mean, you're healthy and all that stuff?" Alfie wanted to ask if having had a breast removed affected her ability to have children. Gussie anticipated her question.

"Alfie, honey, you don't have to feel embarrassed. You can ask me. The doctor says I'm healthy as a horse. The surgery was on my breast, not my female organs. I can have a dozen children. Isn't it wonderful? How's Jim? Tell him when we get there we may decide never to leave." Gussie was on a high. Nothing could lower her spirits. Alfie decided not to mention her uncomfortable feeling of being watched. She laughed to herself at the thought. Her nerves must be in worse shape than she realized. They said their good-byes. Alfie could barely stand the wait until their arrival. Lou was about the only person who seemed to sincerely like Jim. She went into the guest room. She had started redecorating and the entire house was in a state of complete upheaval. Hopefully it would be finished before Gussie and Lou arrived. That would keep her occupied. She opened the patio doors and enjoyed the cool ocean breeze on her face.

She called the decorator. He said, "In two weeks? Alfie, are you mad? Have you gone absolutely, stark-raving mad?" She knew how to handle him. "Oh, Calib, I know it's a big job. But my sis and her husband are coming and they live in a mansion and I do so want things to look beautiful. And no one can decorate the way you can. Of course, if you can't finish it, I suppose I could call Jon Dare. He's not as talented as you are but - "I'll do it. I'll do it. I'm not promising I can finish everything, but I'll do what I can. Fair enough? I'll be out around two." Calib stood with his hand still on the phone. It's a good thing he liked Alfie. He would have told anyone else to piss off. But Alfie had class. She also had that good looking hunk of a husband. Calib could hardly control himself, just thinking about Jim made Calib more excited than any man had in a long time. He would be spending long hours at Alfie's with plenty of time to feast his eyes on Jim. He smiled and began gathering his materials and wallpaper. He carried the carpet samples to the car. This was one job he expected to enjoy. Alfie opened the door. Calib smiled. His white teeth sparkled under his deeply tanned face. His light blonde hair was perfectly styled. He wore a tight tank top the color of a watermelon Calvin Klein jeans and sandals coordinated with the small, beige purse which dangled by a loop on his finger. It resembled the small case a man might use to carry around his razor when he traveled. His almond shaped dark brown eyes were fringed with two inch lashes that should have belonged to a woman. Too bad he wanted so much to be one, Alfie thought "What a waste. Calib was so handsome."

"Hi, you're early. Come in." She stepped back as he bent down to gather his materials. He made a second trip to the car for the carpet samples. He closed the door with his foot and looked around. "Early," he said. "I should have been here two months ago." He smiled again. "Okay. I know what wallpaper you want. But look at this carpet sample. I just received it. It's yummy. In the exact color of peach you've been looking for." He watched her face as he held up the square of carpet. "Well?" "I love it. It's perfect. Just perfect. We're going to put this in the dining room and living room only. I want to keep the hardwood floors throughout the rest of the house." He was deep in thought. "Yes, now let me see the bedrooms. Are you still going with the buttercup yellow and lime for the guest room and peach for yours? Or is it the buttercup yellow and lime for your room?"

Soon they were in the kitchen. Alfie looked at the clock. "Oh, no. I've got to dress. Just go ahead and do whatever you have to do. Jim's taking me to dinner. I only have an hour before he gets here." She rushed into the bedroom, stripping off her clothes. She reached into the shower and turned the water on. What was she going to wear? The fine, cool spray from the shower relaxed her. She closed her eyes and let the water hit her face. She wrapped the fluffy white towel around her and went to the closet. She took out a mint off the shoulder dress and matching sandals. The room felt stuffy. She stepped over to the patio doors and opened them. She marveled at the beautiful pink and orange sunset draped over the blue ocean and the waves with their soft whitecaps. She felt tranquil, almost sedated. Someone was watching her. She turned her head quickly. A figure of a man stepped around the corner of the house. She knew it wasn't Calib. The man had a hat on and his clothes were one color. Sort of a dirty gray.

Alfie stood there paralyzed. She closed the patio doors and removed the towel. She walked back into her bathroom and creamed her body. Should she call Jeff and report the incident or forget it? She knew now she was quite sane. Someone was watching her. If the man had wanted to harm her, he could have. Why did he want to stand and look at her? None of it made sense. She finished dressing. She heard Jim's voice. Taking a quick look in the mirror, she smiled. The mint green brought out her emerald green eyes. Calib's partner, Lenny, had arrived. They were holding up strips of wallpaper and laying it beside the peach carpet. Jim stood with a drink in his hand, trying to act interested in the color scheme as Calib asked his opinion on one color. Lenny screamed, "This is it. Just look at this marvelous color." He held it next to the carpet. It was perfect. Alfie smiled. Lenny was one of the most meticulous people she had ever known. Everything had to be just so. He would go to extremes until he threw himself into a tizzy. Calib treasured his opinions and style. They were perfect together. What one didn't think of, the other one did. Calib squealed, "Oh, Lenny. That's absolutely perfect. What would I ever do without you?" Lenny's face lit up like a neon sign. Now Calib said, "Let's tackle that horrible kitchen." Lenny's eyes rolled to the side and he laughed.

"That will take a week." They both looked at Alfie and Calib said, "You two have a good time. You won't mind if we raid your fridge later, will you?" Not waiting for an answer, they picked up some materials and walked into the kitchen, still discussing that horrible tile.

The drive was peaceful. Neat little buildings came into sight. The streets were empty except for a few window shoppers. The parking lot was full as they passed the town's new gourmet restaurant, The Lobster House. The Lobster House catered to the younger crowd on week ends because of the disco dancing. A beautiful cocktail lounge and dance floor connected to the dining area. A band for the more settled couples entertained there Sunday through Thursday. Then there was the disco on Friday and Saturday. It was a gold mine. Alfie's building sat on the corner next to Darwell's Paint and Hardware Store. The sign swayed in the breeze. The Castle House. Every time Alfie passed or visited the store she wished Guy and Uncle Will could see it. They would both be so proud.

They were going to Jonas'. Jonas' sat at the edge of town on the wharf. It had been there forever and was Alfie's favorite place. It had been built from redwood that had turned blue-gray from the salt air. Redwood tables decorated the inside. Huge fishing nets hung on the walls. Lanterns on each table gave off a soft light. The room was warmed by a roaring fireplace that covered one entire wall. They pulled into the parking lot. Old and new fishing boats lined the wharf. A strong smell of fish filled the air. Jim opened her door. Alfie stood and looked at the ocean that now looked black under the full moon. Alfie's mind raced back in time. She and Guy were standing on the wharf laughing, their stomachs full from their favorite meal, squid. The love they felt for each other shining on their faces. People smiled at them as they passed by. She felt that horrible ache in her chest. Jim's voice cut into her thoughts. "Hey, are we gonna stand out here all night?" He guided her inside.

Marlene took their drink order. Marlene had been the waitress here as long as Alfie could remember. She was about 45 with the body of a 20 year old and the face of a 50 year old. He face was heavily lined around her eyes and mouth. She was always dark brown and leathery from the sun. She and her husband, Hank, owned a sailboat and they took it out every day. Hank had children from a previous marriage, but they rarely came to visit any more now that they were both in college. One would soon have an M.D. degree and the other a CPA He was tremendously proud of them. He being a retired fisherman, Hank marveled at the fact that his children had chosen such ambitious pursuits. Hank claimed that his ex-wife and her family deserved all the credit. Marlene was equally proud. She was unable to bear children and she thought of Hank's as her own. The kids felt the same way about her. Marlene brought their drinks back. "I heated the brandy for you." She sat the brandy in front of Alfie. She took a lemon twist and rubbed it around the edge of the brandy glass then let it fall in. Jim raised the Beefeaters to his lips taking a long drink. He said, "looks like business is slow." His eyes took in the other two couples."Shhh, don't say that too loud. I don't want Jason to go into a rage. The Lobster House has really hurt us. They even tried to get me to work for them. But I would never do that to Jason."

"I love it here," Alfie said. "This is my favorite place." "I wish everyone felt that way. People forget that when times were hard, Jason used to feed them for nothing. He took a loss because they were his friends. Now half of those people go to the Lobster House." Marlene shook her head. "Do you need more time before you order?" "I know what I want," Alfie said looking at Jim. "Do you?" "Yeah, I'm ready. I'll have the lobster. Bleu cheese on my salad." Jim pointed at Alfie. "Your turn." "The same, but I want escargot and no salad," Alfie said.as she stood up, "I'll be right back." Alfie walked toward the back where the powder room was. A man was seated in the very back at the last table. A hat was pulled down over his eyes. He wore a beard, but somehow seemed familiar. She pushed the thought out of her mind and started into the bathroom. It hit her. This was the man she had seen standing at the corner of the house. He also wore a beard. This man, however, was not dressed shabbily. Could it be the same man? She walked out of the bathroom.

The man was making his way toward the front. He was limping. She stood and watched him. He turned as if he could feel her staring. He looked at her for a moment, then turned and disappeared through the front door. Her heart hammered in her chest. Who was he? Why was he watching her? Or was he the one? She couldn't be sure. She slid into the booth. She raised the brandy up to her lips and took a long drink. The brandy burned, causing her eyes to water. The warmness spread. "You look like you saw a ghost. You okay? Jim looked at Alfie's face. "I'm a little tired, that's all." Why didn't she tell him? Something held her back. Jim stood up and bowed. "May I have this dance?" One of Nat King Cole's songs was playing,

"Unforgettable." One of her favorites.Their bodies swayed to the music. Marlene passed. Jim reached out and caught the tail of her blouse then held up two fingers. When they reached the table, Marlene had arrived with their drinks andAlfie's escargot. Alfie picked at her food. "Well, what do you think?"

Alfie looked up. Jim was waiting for her to answer and she hadn't even heard his question. "What? I'm sorry, Jim. I was thinking about Calib and Lenny. I was wondering what they decided for the kitchen. What did you ask?" "I said what do you think about our selling the fishing boats and just concentrating on the store?" Sell the fishing boats? What was he talking about? Guy loved those boats. "Why, are you having problems with the men?" She waited for him to answer. He stared at his glass, rubbing the rim with his finger. "You know I don't have the same feeling for the sea as you people. We don't need the money. We don't even need the store. We could go to Europe, or even China. Anywhere you want to go. Let's travel." The truth was that he was getting restless. He had seen enough of this quiet and peaceful life. It was fine for a while. He had everything he had wanted. Eventually he would leave. He wanted Alfie with him. He seemed never to tire of her company. He had risked much to have her and had no intention of losing her now. Alfie looked into his eyes. She shivered. There was a hardness in them that frightened her. "I'm happy here, Jim. I don't want to travel. Not now. Maybe I'll change my mind one day. I love this island and there's Uncle Frank's age to consider. Something could happen to him anytime and I would want to be here. And, I haven't told you this, but Gussie's pregnant. I want to be around when her baby is born. There's so much." She sighed. "Don't worry. We'll talk about it later. There's no rush. I understand how you feel." He didn't understand. He would let it go for a couple of weeks. He would have his way somehow. He paid the check.

They rode up the quiet street. He turned into the parking lot of the store. "Just want to pick up the ledgers. I won't be a minute." One street lamp dimly lit the corner. She started to lay her head back on the seat. There was someone standing at the corner of the building. A man wearing a hat. She screamed, "Jim." Jim ran toward the car. She pointed toward the corner of the building. "There was a man standing there." Jim reached through her window and opened the glove compartment. He picked the gun up, released the safety and ran toward the corner of the building. He walked back to the car, ledgers still in his hand. "Whoever it was is gone now. Probably some bum passing through." "How could he disappear so quickly? Where did he go?" She waited. He didn't answer. "Well, where did he go?" "He probably didn't go anywhere. It's dark around there. He could be hiding. I'll give Jesse a call when we get home. Will that make you feel better?" He smiled and squeezed her knee. She gazed out the window. It was the same man. She was almost sure of it. Jim hung up the phone. "Jesse said he'll send someone over there now and the patrol will give the store special attention for a couple of weeks." Alfie slid between the cool sheets.

"Hmm, that's good." Maybe they would catch him. She was asleep before Jim could get in bed.

She opened her eyes. She felt the dull throb in her temples. She never could drink. Two drinks and she was sick. The shrill ring of the phone didn't help. It was Lenny. "Rise and shine, luv. Calib and I are on our way out. There's a lot to do and so little time to do it. See you in half an hour." She looked at the clock, 8:30. She swung herself to a sitting position on the side of the bed. Some cold juice and aspirin would do wonders. Her eyes rested on the knobs of the patio door. They were turning slowly back and forth. Alfie's heart seemed to stop. She opened the drawer of her nightstand and placed her hand on the cold steel of her 25 automatic. She stood on the cool hardwood floor. She placed her feet slowly one in front of the other. The phone crashed to the floor. She looked down. The cord was wrapped around her ankle. "Oh No " She kicked her foot free and ran to the doors, swinging them open. A man with a limp and a hat pulled over his eyes was making his way toward the pier. Alfie walked over to the phone and dialed Jesse's number. Calib and Lenny arrived, both dressed in Bermuda shorts and tank tops. Lenny was as dark as Calib was. They went straight into the kitchen. "Alfie, you will walk on pink marble floors. Just look at this color." Lenny placed the marble slab on the floor. It was beautiful. A creamy pink. Alfie smiled. "It's beautiful. Just perfect." The chimes sounded for the front door. That had to be Jesse. Alfie excused herself to answer the door. Alfie had slipped on a pair of shorts and a halter top. Her feet were bare. She hated wearing shoes in the house.

She opened the door. Jesse's grin lit up his whole face. He had enough teeth for two mouths. His ruddy complexion was covered with a million freckles. His hair was bright red, thick and unruly. He stood about six feet six inches tall and his muscles pushed at the seams of his uniform. He always gave the appearance of being just scrubbed. He bent down and kissed her cheek. She put her arm around his waist and guided him to the sofa. He made himself comfortable as she poured coffee for both of them. "I know you didn't call me out here just for coffee. What's wrong?" Alfie took a sip of her coffee, then sat it on the table. She looked at Jesse. The cup looked like a child's toy in his massive hands. "Jesse, someone's watching me." She told him the feeling she had of being watched, about the man with the limp at Jonas', and reminded him about the incident last night at their store. Jesse started to speak. Alfie held up her hand. "Jesse this morning someone was trying to open the patio doors to my bedroom. I got the gun from the nightstand, but my foot got hung in the phone cord and the crash of the phone scared whoever it was away. When I looked outside, I saw a man walking toward the pier. Jesse, the man had a limp and wore a hat pulled over his face, just like the man I saw at Jonas'." The worried look on Jesse's face scared Alfie. "Have you called Jim and told him about this?" Alfie shook her head. "I hesitated to mention it to any one because I thought maybe it was only my imagination. I'm not scared Jesse, The man I saw at Jonas' seemed familiar somehow. There was something about him that I can't explain. I just want to know why he's watching me."

"Alfie, I don't want to scare you but we just found the body of a young woman at the far end of the pier." "She had been raped and beaten," Jesse paused, "beaten to death." "Oh, God," Alfie's hand covered her mouth. She was going to be sick. Jesse called Jim. Jim placed another cool cloth on her head. "Why didn't you tell me you felt you were being watched. Why?" Jim could not conceal the anger in his voice. "Jim, don't be angry with me, please. I wasn't sure until this morning." Jim ran his hand through his hair. He sat on the edge of the bed. "For God's sake, why do you want to know for sure? What did the woman know for sure that was found under the pier?" His head rested on the palms of his hands as he rubbed his eyes. Alfie touched his shoulder. He turned and gathered her into his arms. Just the thought of anything happening to her made him a little crazy. Maybe he did love her after all. Why else would he feel this way. Jesse stood in the doorway watching. He cleared his throat. Jim released Alfie. Alfie lay back on the pillows. He tucked the covers around her, kissing her lips. They walked out onto the patio. Jim filled his pipe, the tobacco felt damp. The sweet aroma from the tobacco filled Alfie's nostrils and gave her a feeling of security.

Both men sat silently, each absorbed in his own thoughts. Jim broke the silence. "I had no idea. She didn't tell me anything." "Women are funny, Jim. And we don't know for sure that she is being watched." Jim poured more gin over his ice cubes. "You ready, Jesse?" Jesse held his glass up. "Yeah, I'll have one more." Jay and Cassie reached the patio. Jim and Jesse stood up. The men exchanged handshakes. Soon everyone was seated with a drink. "What's going on Jim? When you guys didn't show up for our card game, we started worrying. Then we saw Jesse's car here all afternoon. And, well, we're your friends. If there's anything wrong and we can help, here we are. And if we're being too nosy and it's none of our business, tell us that, too." "Thanks, Jay. Maybe you can help." When Jim finished filling them in on everything, Cassie's face had taken on an ashen color. "If you see anyone that looks suspicious to you, call me. Anyone that's new or looks as if they might be snooping. Okay?" Jesse stood, hoping they would all take this seriously. "I'm leaving Kyle here tonight. Someone will relieve him in the morning. There will be a man here 24-hours a day, at least for a couple of weeks. I'm going to get to the bottom of this."

Jim locked the front door after Jesse. Jay was filling his glass when Jim walked back into the living room. "Cassie went to check on Alfie. I'll have Cassie check on her throughout the day. If you think of anything we can do, just ask." Cassie walked back into the room. "She's asleep. I'm so worried and I feel so helpless." She didn't mention that Alfie had already confided in her about this. Jim turned out the lights and checked the outside flood lights to make sure they were on. Kyle sat in his patrol car, watching the house. This was about the most excitement he'd seen since he joined the small Sheriff's Department on Pink Shell Island. Jesse was probably one of the brightest men Kyle had ever known. Politics didn't run the Sheriff's office, Jesse did and he ran it by the book. Pink Shell Island had never had any major problems. Everyone respected Jesse and knew he meant business. There were no bums and drunks hanging around. Troublemakers were given a second chance, but never a third. He had watched families pack up and move because one of theirs refused to mend his ways. Kyle had been accepted by Jesse because Jesse had watched him grow up and knew what kind of man Kyle was. Kyle had always had a love for law and order and Jesse knew this, too. Kyle opened the door of the patrol car, stood up and stretched. He thought of Jill. God, he loved her. He loved her petite, size-three frame, her long, jet-black hair and her eyes which were almost the same color as her hair. Kyle was blonde with blue eyes. He was six foot three, slender, yet muscular. Their appearances complimented each other.

He sighed and started walking. The night was peaceful. The ocean had a calming effect on him. Kyle rested his hand on his gun.

chapter twenty two

THE DREAM

ALFIE'S EYES FLUTTERED. SHE was dreaming. She dreamed of rainbows, thunder and long dark tunnels. Huge black waves engulfed her as she went deeper into sleep. Little men dressed in funny suits of every color in the rainbow pinched and pulled at her skin and hair. They were laughing and talking in a language that she could not understand. They were pulling her through the sand and into the waves. They wanted to drown her. Yes, they wanted her dead and there was nothing she could do to stop them. The fear she felt was so real she could taste the bile coming up into her throat. Then an explosion, so great, it shook the earth and the waters parted. The Old Man in the Sea rose and stood like a giant over the earth. His snow white hair and beard gave off a luminous glow. His hand reached down and scooped her up. The little men in their funny suits fell dead and the waves washed them out to sea. The fire in his eyes warned her of danger ahead.

She opened her eyes. Her body was drenched with sweat. She was trembling. She felt next to her for Jim, but he wasn't there. She jumped out of bed, pulled the wet gown over her head and reached for her robe. She put her hand to her hair which was soaking. How could she have perspired that much? The moon lit the room. She followed the sweet smell of Jim's pipe to the patio. He sat on a lounge chair, deep in thought. Smoke poured from his pipe as he sucked hard to keep the fire going. His huge frame seemed to fill the patio. His rugged, handsome features were complimented by his dark curly hair and olive complexion. His shirt was open, showing his chest. His hand gripped the pipe. A muscle twitched in his cheek.

She walked over and sat in the chair next to him. A small white wrought iron table separated the two chairs. She glanced down at the picture that lay on the table. She felt a wave of nausea. The picture was of herself and Guy. She had had Jim snap it of them just before their boat had sailed the last time she had seen Guy alive. How did it get here? The picture had been taken with an instant Polaroid and Guy had put the picture in his pocket. There were no negatives. That was the last she had seen of Guy or the picture. What was going on? There had to be a logical explanation for this. Jim had stood up and was tapping his pipe against the block wall, allowing the remaining tobacco to blow away in the breeze. He spoke without turning around. "Someone's playing tricks Alfie. That picture was laying on the table when I came out here tonight. I remember taking it of you and Guy." "Why is this happening Jim, why?" She was trembling. Jim lifted her out of the chair into his arms. He held her tight. He could feel her tears on his neck.

chapter twenty three

THE RUDE AWAKENING

ANTHONY SAT ON THE edge of the small bed. The walls of the adobe house felt hot. He knew it was probably 110 degrees outside. Marie Sanchez stood at the stove stirring a big pot of frijoles. She covered the pot and turned her attention to the stack of tortilla's she had just made. She wrapped them in two white cloth towels. There she thought, the meal' was almost ready. The green chilies and pork needed to cook at least another half hour. She would check on Anthony. Anthony wanted to stand regardless of the fact his right leg was gone, he still felt whole. He stared at the blank space from his knee down. Today Dr. Vega would fit him for a leg. If only he could remember what had happened. One thing he knew for sure he could never repay Maria and Jose Sanchez for all that they had done for him. He owed them his life.

Jose was a warm, kind-hearted man who lived for each day as it arose. He had spent his 55 years helping everyone he could. His heart went out to anyone he thought to be in need. His wife Maria was the same way. They were never blessed with children so they played father and mother to everyone. Their family and friends thought one of them would surely be canonized for sainthood. The deep waters of the Pacific were cold as Jose and his two friends fished. Jose held up his hands and shouted "Juan, stop the boat! Stop! Look over there it's a man floating on the driftwood." "No," Juan said. "That's not a man." They cut the motor of the boat as Jose lowered himself into the water. He pushed the driftwood and the man to the boat. The three men managed to get the half-dead form aboard. The color drained from Jose's face "Heavenly Father, I think he is already dead. Hurry Juan this poor man must have a doctor." Carlos Lopez knelt with Jose Sanchez and prayed. It seemed to be the only thing they could do for this poor gringo. Juan radioed ahead for help. The doctors shook their heads as they worked fiendishly to save the gringo. He had lost too much blood. Why the shark hadn't finished the job, nobody knew. Jose rushed home to tell Maria. Maria went to the church to light candles and pray for the poor gringo.

Jose and Maria spent weeks at the hospital. Jose had taken responsibility for the gringo. Their friends and family said nothing.There would be no prejudice shown to the gringo. If Jose and Maria thought he was okay and wanted to help him, they would help him. It was as simple as that. Jose decided to give the gringo a name. He had no identification and he was still in a coma. He gave it great thought and decided that St. Anthony had helped to pull the gringo through, and that his name should be Anthony. Anthony remained in a coma. Maria kept fresh flowers in his room. She talked to him because the doctor said he could hear even if he was not awake. Jose, Maria, their family and friends took turns at the hospital talking to Anthony. The doctors said it was a miracle that he lived and told them not to expect much more. Eight months later, Jose and Maria were at Anthony's bedside. Maria was reading to Anthony from the Bible, the 23rd Psalm. Anthony's eyelids fluttered and opened. He looked at the two people who stood before him. His face was a blank.

Maria started crying. Jose leaned over and hugged Anthony. He too was crying. Anthony remembered nothing...amnesia the doctors said. He might never remember his past. Jose and Maria took Anthony home to live with them. Where else was he going to live? They cared for him as if he were their own son. Maria thought that Anthony was boo-ti-ful, with his ice blue eyes and hair just the color of wheat. She babied and pampered him heaping the love upon him that she would have given to her own child. Her heart especially went out to him when she heard him sobbing during the night. Jose at first did not interfere but tried to think of something he could say or do to help. He sat on the side of Anthony's bed. "For me to tell you that I know how you feel would be a lie if I had gone through the terrible ordeal that you did I'm sure it would have killed me. You are a very brave and strong person. Somewhere you have family that miss you very much. I do not believe your memory of the past is lost forever. One day you will remember everything but for now you need help and Maria and I want to help you." Anthony looked at this small, old man. His hands were brown and callused from hard, honest work. His head was covered with white hair. His dark brown eyes were full of warmth and understanding.

"I feel that I'm a burden to you. You and Maria have already done too much for me how can I every repay your generosity and kindness I'm only half a man. And now you want to buy me a leg. How can I let you spend your hard earned money on me anymore? Why didn't I die? Why?" He beat his fist on the bed. The gentle face of Jose Sanchez contorted in anger. "How can you be so selfish? Your suffering has been great but you are not the only one that has suffered." Jose paused. "When I was a young man, before I ever met Maria, I was married and had a son I lived in Chihuahua. The town was ruled by the banditos. My wife Carmen, was very beautiful. "Pedro Perez, was the second man in charge of the banditos he wanted my wife. He went to my home one day while I was working and tried to rape her. She got away and locked herself in the bathroom. When she told me I took a gun and went after him. When I found him he was alone. I told him if he ever came around my wife again, I would kill him. I should have killed him then."

Jose walked over to the window and stood staring into the sky. His shoulders seemed to slump. The anger had left his face and a look of pain had taken its place. He continued, his voice now low. I told Carmen that I had taken care of everything. But Carmen could see in my eyes that I didn't believe it any more than she did. The banditos would be back. They were a gang of blood thirsty unfeeling savages. Carmen and I lived with that fear every day. One night I arrived at home to find our front yard covered with hoof prints. Carmen had been raped and beaten to death. I found my son outside next to the house. The horses had trampled him, I went crazy. I didn't know a person could hurt the way I did. To join my family in death would have been a blessing. I knew where the banditos went to drink. I went to the cantina and I hid in back. I waited for many hours before Pedro came out. When he and four of his men came around back to get their horses I shot them all. The banditos numbered over 100 and I knew when they discovered their friends had been killed it would not be long before they came after me. So I got on my horse and left. I have never returned to Chihuahua again. If it had not been for Maria, I would have lost my mind. I wondered why my family had to die. And you tell me you don't know why you were allowed to live. Life is precious just thank God every day that you wake up. When you are well I will let you help me on the fishing boats. That is how you can repay us. But do not think that you are only half a man. Being a man has nothing to do with your leg. A man is measured by what is in his heart. Jose turned and walked from the room and closed the door softly behind him. Anthony slept a deep and peaceful sleep.

Maria walked into Anthony's bedroom to find him staring at his leg. "Anthony, Dr. Vega will be here shortly are you excited?" Maria's face beamed. She walked over to Anthony and gave him a hug. Anthony grinned. He had come to love Maria like a mother. He had no memory of his own mother or father. Was he married? Did he have children? No, the thought of walking on an artificial leg did not excite him. But he said, "More than you'll every know Maria, more than you'll ever know." He squeezed her hand. Walking on the leg was at first exhausting and extremely painful, but gradually the pain was reduced to a dull throb. Anthony had won one more battle.

chapter twenty four

REMEMBERING

STANDING ON THE WHARF and looking out at the ocean gave Anthony a peaceful feeling. Looking at Jose's two 30-foot fishing boats tugged at a memory that stayed just out of reach. "Come on, gringo. Are you gonna work today?" Jose and Carlos laughed as Anthony made his way unsteadily up the plank of the old boat. He balanced himself with a cane. Sweat ran down his face as he worked beside the other men. Jose walked over and placed his hand on Anthony's arm. "Sit down rest, this is your first day back at work not your last amigo." Anthony was grateful for the few minutes of rest. The throbbing pain in his leg eased slightly. As he stared at the fishing nets being lifted out of the water he saw a fleeting illusion of a smiling girl with short curly red hair. Her skin bronzed and her eyes were the color of emeralds. His heart raced for an instant then the image vanished. It had been 14 months since he had been pulled from the ocean. He mentioned nothing of his fleeting vision but Anthony knew that his lost past was beginning to return to him at last. He lay in bed exhausted. He had remembered nothing more of his past since the flashback of the girl a week ago. He rubbed his thick bearded chin. He was happy on the fishing boats. Perhaps he had been a fisherman. Sleep claimed his thoughts.

chapter twenty five

TRINA

TRINA STOOD IN THE doorway. She was the daughter of
Juan Chavez. The morning sun made her jet black
waist length hair shine. Her face lit up as Anthony
entered the kitchen. Her thick Mexican accent made
it hard for him to understand her. "I thought you
no gonna get up I make chorizo," she pointed to the
stove. "For you." She was a pretty girl. She had a
small, straight nose full lips and round eyes so dark
brown they were almost black. Her figure was a little
too full, but not bad to look at. Anthony said, "Thank
you chorizo is my favorite breakfast. But you must eat
with me." He held out his hand. She smiled shyly and
lowered her eyes. She reached out and took his hand.
She was there every day waiting for him. She would
remove his shoe and help him unstrap his artificial
leg. She massaged his neck and back waiting on him
hand and foot. He had begun to find her presence

extremely comforting. One Sunday morning he was sleeping late. Maria had covered the window in his room with a dark heavy material to keep the sun out and the room was cool even at 10 a.m. He felt someone kiss his cheek he thought he was dreaming. Breasts rubbed against his chest he knew it was Trina before he opened his eyes. His hands followed the curve of her body. His mouth found hers, guilt swept over him. But not enough guilt to push her away..

The boats unloaded the tuna. The catch had been better than Jose could ever remember. Anthony was like a lucky charm. With Anthony's advice Jose had made a few changes in his fishing business and his money had increased beyond anything he could imagine. And Anthony could not have been happier for this kind generous man who deserved even more. Anthony had a strength and a self-assuredness on the boats that had gained for him the respect of the local fishermen. But, for some reason, he could not feel happy here. His relationship with Trina had started to feel suffocating. Until he regained his past, he could make no commitments to the future. He lounged in an antique bathtub with his head situated comfortably on a folded towel. He opened his eyes. The sun had disappeared, oh, no! I must have dozed off. How inconsiderate of me to take this long in the tub. Why hadn't Jose or Maria pounded on the door? But he knew they would never disturb him. Anything he did was all right with them. He pushed himself up on his one leg and turned slowly to reach for a towel. The one that had cushioned his head lay in the water. His foot slipped. The loud crunch of his head against the tub relieved Anthony of any more thoughts.

They pushed their chairs back from the table. "I'll have to diet for a year," Alfie patted her stomach. "Yeah, that was the best meal I've had in a long time, Cassie," Jim said. He caught the irritated look on Alfie's face and grinned. Jay was out of his chair. "Brandy and coffee on the patio? I'll get the coffee. Jim can get the brandy." And Cassie said, "I'll check on the kids."Alfie followed Cassie. "I haven't seen the kids in a long time." She realized it had only been a week. She couldn't believe it. So much had happened in a week. Cassie opened the door to Ginny's room. Jay, Jr. and Ginny sat on the floor. They were absorbed in their new game "Risk." Ginny looked up and smiled. She was a beautiful child with jet black hair and blue eyes. Her complexion was cream colored coffee. At twelve she looked fourteen. A lot of hearts would be broken by her no second thoughts on that. Jay, Jr., age nine, had a fair complexion. His skin seemed almost transparent. His sandy hair contrasted sharply with his deep brown eyes and gave him a fragile look. He was almost too pretty to be a boy. Both children were bright and well behaved. The kind of children Alfie would want...if ever she did want children. Raising children was something that seemed better suited to people like Cassie. Ginny and Jay were up off the floor in a flash. They wrapped their arms around Alfie as she returned their hugs. They pulled her over to the game showing her how to play.

"Oh, no," Cassie said. "It's time both of you got ready for bed. We grown ups have a lot to talk about." She hugged both of them. "Tell you what," Alfie said, "if it's okay with your mom you can bring the game over to my house one day this week and teach me how to play. Okay?" They both readily agreed. After checking the windows in their rooms they said their final goodnights. The men sipped their brandy. "Did they ever find the man with the limp?" Jim shook his head. "No, and they haven't found anything else. Nothing but peace and quiet. I hope it's not the lull before the storm. Alfie's not too happy having a deputy with her every second of the day. She's ready to tell Jesse she doesn't need them."

"Are you going to let her do that?" Jay couldn't hide the irritation in his voice. He felt that all serious decisions should be left up to the man. He really liked Alfie and conceded that Jim was okay. There was something about him he couldn't quite pin down. Something he was hiding. "Well, are you?" "No, I'm not," Jim said. "I talked to Jesse this morning. Regardless of what Alfie says, Jesse will have her followed without her knowing it if he has to." Jay sat back. "Good." He smiled as he drained his glass. Jay wanted everyone he liked to be protected. He was probably the best family man on Pink Shell Island. A perfect lumberjack type with a booming voice that scared everyone who didn't know him. His jet black hair and dark blue eyes along with sparkling white teeth had him dubbed as a ladies' man by people who didn't know him. Alfie always said he was just like a pussycat. Jay worked on the Hugh Fishing Boats. Cassie had taught kindergarten until her failing health had forced her to give it up. She welcomed the extra time to spend with her children.

The days passed quickly. Alfie watched as Calib and Lenny transformed her house into a showroom spectacular. Everything was done in peach and cream with splashes of lime and buttercup yellow. She bought a new wardrobe all in pastels. She even found time to spend on the beach with Ginny and Jay, Jr., building sandcastles and learning to play their games. Her body darkened to a golden-brown. She and Jim spent time with Jay and Cassie fishing off the pier, having barbecues on the beach, dining at Jonas' in town. Alfie even spent time helping out at the store. But Jim's attitude toward her had begun to change and he began to spend more time on the boats and at the store. She seemed to spend much of her time alone. She welcomed Old Sarge telling of his experiences and how the "Old Man in the Sea" had saved his life so many times. Her love for the ocean became even stronger and for the "Old Man in the Sea."After all she had missed the fantasy in her life or was it fantasy?.

chapter twenty six

THE LULL

TWO WEEKS PASSED WITH no incident. Alfie's 24-hour guard had been stopped. Things were back to normal, or so it seemed. Gussie and Lou would arrive at 11:40. Good grief, Alfie would have to hurry. She slipped the pink dress over her head. Her strawberry hair had turned lighter from the sun. Her green eyes were startling next to her golden-brown skin. She dabbed a little peach color on her cheeks and lips. There, that would have to do. She slipped her feet into her almost-strapless sandals. They were made from the softest leather and dyed to match her dress. The airport was small. But today it seemed unusually crowded. She looked at her watch. She had made it with ten minutes to spare. As the passengers began coming through the door, Alfie looked at each face. She spotted the carefully groomed head towering a little above the others. Yes, there she was. Every hair in place. Her three inch nails were perfect. They both squealed at the same time. Then they were hugging each other. "Let me look at you. Stand back. You look great. Absolutely great." Alfie squealed again.

She spotted Lou wrestling with the luggage and ran to hug him. "You look great, too," Gussie said. I'm so glad to be here. It seems like ten years since I've seen you. Look at that tan. You must live on the beach. We've got so much to talk about. Where do we start?" Gussie laughed as she squeezed her sister and Lou. "What did you and Lou do, move?" Alfie laughed looking at five suitcases and a large overnight case. Gussie grinned. "You know how I am when I travel." "I just hope I can fit all of them in my car." Alfie's custom Rolls Royce convertible was not really designed for hauling luggage. When, finally, everything was packed carefully into the car, there wasn't a square inch of unused space. "I had forgotten how beautiful this place is. It's breathtaking." As they drove home Gussie's eyes took in the beauty of the blue ocean and white sand, the trees heavy with beautiful colored flowers, and the smell of the ocean filled her nostrils and calmed her soul.

Alfie pulled up in the driveway. She unlocked the door. "Well, here we are. How do you like it? I changed a few things." "Oh, Alfie! Everything's gorgeous. You've changed the whole house I love it, I simply love it." Alfie took her into the guest room. The soft breeze from the window gently blew the cream-colored sheer curtains. A cream-colored down comforter covered the soft-peach bedspread. The dark mahogany furniture smelled of lemon. The hardwood floor glistened. A thick, fluffy peach rug lay on the floor next to the bed. Hanging on the wall above the bed there was a picture of a clown. He was sitting on a large ball which hung in mid-air and tears were spilling from his eyes as he gazed down on a raging ocean. Gussie's eyes saw everything. You could have heard a pin drop. "Guy painted that picture for you, didn't he?" Alfie nodded her head, yes. She could feel that lump in her throat, that old familiar urge to cry. She just couldn't break down. That was all in the past. She gained control of herself, clearing her throat, she smiled. "Tell you what, I'll help you unpack. We have a big night planned for you two, so maybe you should take a nap. You must be tired after that long plane ride. I'll fix you something tall and cold while you shower, okay?" She was out of the room before Gussie or Lou could say a word. Gussie knew she would not mention Guy's name again, not this trip. Alfie's wounds were still unhealed. They pushed the short legged beach chairs into the sand. Gussie plopped down in one. Alfie handed her a tall frosted glass containing pineapple orange juice and light rum topped with a squeeze of lime. Gussie sucked the sweet liquid through a plastic straw it tasted great! She looked at the surfers among the breakers. How easy they made it look. The sound of the surf was soothing. Seagulls flew over head. She wanted to stay here forever.

Jim and Jay were busy getting everything ready to barbecue. The thick pieces of red meat had been marinated overnight. A large bowl held green peppers and onions that would be put on the skewers with the meat. The refrigerator held a tossed salad and potato salad; loaves of Italian bread waited to be popped into the oven. Cassie sat down next to Gussie. "You look great," Cassie said. "I'm so glad you're here." She squeezed Gussie's hand. "Thanks. So am I. Those kids of yours have grown a foot. It hasn't been that long. So why do I feel so guilty? Tell me what's going on? Fill me in on some of it." Gussie shifted in the small chair. She looked bigger than she had before. Old Sarge had walked up behind them. "Go ahead and tell her Cassie she should know. I'll go and help Alfie." After listening to Cassie, Gussie was silent for a few moments. "How do they know that everything is okay now? Where's Jesse? That's who I want to talk to." Gussie looked around. Jesse had just arrived. His new girlfriend was holding on to his arm for dear life. He certainly wasn't getting away. Gussie laughed to herself. Jesse had on white shorts and a green tank top with brown leather Italian sandals. His little girlfriend had on hot-pink short-shorts with a tiny halter top from which her big boobs pushed to get free. Gussie noticed her reason for holding on to Jesse so tightly...spike heels were sinking deep into the sand with every step she took. Spike heels on the beach! Gussie and Cassie looked at each other. Cassie had to turn and walk away or burst out laughing. Cassie grabbed her stomach. She walked slowly toward her house. She would not be able to get through the evening without the pain pills.

Gussie smiled. Jesse pushed his girlfriend's hand off of his arm and grabbed Gussie in a big bear-hug.

"Why do you look better every time I see you.?" He patted her stomach, " What do we have here?" Jesse made a growling sound and nipped at her ear. Gussie laughed as she said, "you'er an animal.". Jesse put this arm around the girl's waist. "Gussie, this is Kim. Kim's visiting from Arkansas." Gussie held out her hand. Kim took it, smiling timidly. Why, she's shy and scared, thought Gussie. "I'm borrowing Kim for a minute. Go join the men." She helped guide Kim to the patio of the house. Alfie was coming out of the kitchen with a big bowl in her hand. Sarge was following with paper plates and napkins. Lou was mixing a fresh batch of pina coladas. Alfie sat the bowl on the redwood table. She smiled at Kim. "You must be Jesse's friend. I'm Alfie and this is Sarge, an old friend of the family. And this is Lou, Gussie's husband."

"Pleased to meet you all." Kim's southern drawl was so thick you could cut it with a knife. Alfie's eyes rested on Kim's spike heels and then caught Gussie's eye. "I was just showing Kim the powder room. We'll be right back." Gussie smiled and hurried Kim into the house. She heard Kim gasp, "Oh, my gawd. This is the most beautiful house I've ever seen. I can't believe it. I just can't believe it." Her eyes took in the front room. The thick peach carpet sank under each step. Gussie laughed. "Yes, it is beautiful, isn't it. My sister has a flair for decorating." None of Gussie's shoes fit Kim. "Come on, follow me. We'll look in Alfie's closet. She won't mind." Gussie grabbed Kim's arm and pulled her along. Alfie's room was unbelievable. The walls were covered with flocked wallpaper of the palest yellow. The dark pecan furniture glistened. The huge four poster bed was topped with a buttercup yellow canopy. A thick silk bedspread of the same color covered the bed. A chaise lounge of thick quilted silk, the same pale yellow as the wallpaper, held thick silk throw pillows in lime green, peach and buttercup yellow. A small, round pecan table held a yellow princess phone and an Emmett Kelly clown. Sheer crisscross curtains covered one window, mixing the softest mint green, pale yellow and light peach in to soft swirls of color. It looked as if an artist had taken his brush and made soft strokes all over the curtain. Two French doors led out to one side of the patio. Sheer curtains with the same pattern were pulled tight with a small rod on each end, forming close pleats on each French door, covering the small square panes of glass. The shining hardwood floors were covered with thick rugs of buttercup yellow. A dark pecan table sat next to the wall between the window and French doors. On top of it sat an old-fashioned wash basin and water pitcher which were an apple green color. A second yellow princess phone sat on the nightstand beside the bed. Another Emmett Kelly clown sat next to it. There were brass lamps on each nightstand with pale yellow silk shades.

Gussie opened the double doors that led into the giant walk in closet. Rows of shoes lined one wall, every color and style imaginable. "I think we can find something here," Gussie said. "Let's look." She smiled as she waved her hand in front of Kim's eyes. "Hey, are you with me?" Cassie settled the children to making sandcastles and reached into her pocket for her pain pills. The men were busy putting the meat and peppers on the skewers. Alfie finished making fresh drinks for everyone. Gussie and Kim replenished the bowls of potato chips and clam dip. Everyone felt comfortable and happy. Old Sarge stared out at the ocean, biting on his pipe. He felt restless, and an uneasy feeling lay in the pit of his stomach. What he needed to do was talk to the "Old Man in the Sea. Something just didn't feel right.

THE AWAKENING

HE OPENED HIS EYES. His head throbbed. He couldn't think clearly. Where was Alfie? He needed to talk to her. She would tell him why his head hurt so badly.

His eyes focused on Maria. She was wiping her eyes. "Thank God, you are alright." Maria blew her nose into the tissue as she walked over to Anthony and sat on the side of the small bed. "We were so worried. You took a terrible blow to your head. You slipped on the soap. From now on you must call for Jose when you finish your bath. He will help you out of the tub." Anthony hadn't heard a word that Maria had said. He put his hand on hers as he spoke, "My name is Guy. Guy Easterman. I have a home and a wife on Pink Shell Island. I also have my own fishing boats and I want to go home." His voice broke. The tears ran down his face as he raised up and sobbed on Maria's shoulder. "Oh, Maria, I remember everything."

Maria was crying, too. She was happy for Anthony... or Guy. But her heart was saddened at the thought that soon he would leave them. Jose walked into the room. "Carumba, who died?" "Oh, Jose," Maria got up and flew into Jose's arms. "Anthony remembers everything. He's going to leave us." The three cried and hugged each other.

Jose blew his nose. "Enough of that. This is a time to rejoice. Maria, go and light a candle. Anthony and I have a lot to talk about." He swatted her gently on the behind. Jose and Guy talked long into the night. "What if your wife has married again? We should find out some facts before you just walk back into your home. So much time has passed. Your family must surely believe that you are dead." "No," Guy banged his fist on the table. "I don't care if she is married. She is still my wife. And I am going to kill Jim. All of this is his fault. How could I have been so wrong about a person? Why did I trust him, what was I thinking?" Guy dissolved into fresh tears. His body shook with anger and despair as that horrible day ran through his mind.

The boat had turned on its side for the second time. The rope he held onto slipped from his hand as a giant wave engulfed the boat. Someone grabbed his shirt. He held onto that arm with his hands. He looked up into Jim's face. Thank God. Relief flooded through Guy. Wait! What was Jim doing? Jim's legs were wrapped tightly around a pole. His free hand pried Guy's fingers off his arm. The waves continued to cover the deck. Guy held his breath to keep from drowning as he fought to refasten his fingers to Jim's arm. Guy's feet were inches from the ocean. He had no strength left. His eyes met Jim's. He would never forget the smile on Jim's lips and the cold, unfeeling look in his eyes...the last thing that Guy had seen before he slid into the ocean. He had let his body move with the waves, knowing that it was useless to fight against them. He wrapped his arms around a huge piece of driftwood and thought of Jerry. Jerry would know how to get him out of this mess. He felt a searing pain in his head and he welcomed the blackness.

He looked at Jose. "You're right. What do we do first?" Guy thought of Alfie. Maybe seeing him as half a man would disgust her. He could never handle pity. Not from her. Maybe he would stay here and never go back. One person he would contact was Jerry. Jerry would tell him everything that was going on. He told Jose how he felt. Jose was like a father. He understood. They would phone Jerry in the morning. Jose put his arm around Guy's shoulder. "You must pray, my troubled one. Then you will know what to do." Jose sighed. "Now, let us sleep so that we will be able to think more clearly, okay?" Guy shook his head, yes. He felt too drained to even speak.

His dreams were of Alfie. He held her in his arms all night. Her perfume filled his nostrils.

Jerry cried as he listened to Guy's voice on the phone. It was a miracle. There was so much to talk about. Jerry listened to Guy's story. His stomach felt like it had twisted into one big knot. The hate he felt for Jim was overwhelming. One solution - Kill him. Maria put a fresh drink in front of Jerry. She watched the muscle twitch in the side of his face. The same way Jose's face twitched when he was angry. She could feel the strong bond of love between the two brothers. Maria felt like crying again. She took a deep breath and started into the kitchen to cook dinner. After all, Guy may not leave for a few months. Maybe never. She would ask the saints to keep him here.

chapter twenty eight

CHANGES

THE COOL OCEAN BREEZE felt good through the open bedroom window. It was ten p.m. and Jim was still doing the financial ledger for the store. And since he had taken the job of ordering the supplies away from Cole Marshall, he hated to admit it was a bigger job than he had anticipated. Alfie hoped it would take him all night. It made her angry to think he had taken the job away from Cole. Oh, well, why worry about it? He had the extra work, she didn't. Although she had considered looking over the books, Jim's sudden interest made her wonder. He wanted to sell the fishing boats. Maybe he wanted to get rid of the store too. These things were hers long before he arrived on the scene, and his strange actions lately had begun to unnerve her. She would look at the books tomorrow. There. She felt better having made that decision. Her mind drifted to thoughts of Gussie. Only two more months and Alfie would be an aunt. Where had the time gone? And what was wrong with Cassie? She was forever making excuses when Alfie invited her over and she looked horrible. Jay had tried everything to get her to the doctor. Life used to be so simple. What had happened? And Jerry seemed to have dropped out of sight. She had called a million times and he hadn't returned one call. Was he mad at her? She felt like flying to Alaska and finding him. Everything was falling apart. She buried her face into the pillow. Oh, God. If only she could turn the clock back. She missed Guy so much.

It had been only a couple of months since Gussie had seen Alfie. Something was terribly wrong. She could feel it. Gussie hung up the phone. Lou looked at her face. "What's the worried look for? You know darned well that you aren't supposed to worry.. Now, tell me what you want or need and I'll have it sent here in a minute." Lou had walked over to Gussie and cupped her chin with his hand, raising her face to meet his. "Well now, you gonna tell me? Lou's voice had taken on a concerned tone. "Oh, honey. I'm worried about Alfie. Something's wrong. I can tell it. She doesn't want to worry me, but it's in her voice. Is she ever going to be happy again? God knows it isn't money. It has something to do with Jim. Oh, Lou, honey, what can we do? She's all the family I have." "Now, calm down. We can fly down tomorrow and see." Gussie squealed and hugged Lou tightly. "Whoa, now. I won't take you unless you settle down. You have my son to worry about, too, you know. And any undue excitement could upset the apple cart. We only have two months before I'm a papa." "Oh, Lou, I'll do anything you say. I love you so much and I want to have your son. Why couldn't Alfie have found a man like you?"

She laid her head on Lou's chest.

Cassie stared at the ceiling. She knew she couldn't make it out of bed today. Every joint in her body ached and the severe pains in her stomach doubled her over when she tried to stand. She would need a refill for her pain medication soon. Jay thought she had the flu again. He threatened to physically carry her to the doctor if she didn't make an appointment to go. She seemed to grow weaker each day. She knew it was only a matter of time before Jay learned the truth. She couldn't let that happen. Jay and the children had suffered enough. She cried harder as she wiped the tears from her fevered face. The pain was searing her joints like an internal flame. She prayed that God would forgive her as she poured the remaining two-week supply of pain pills into her hand. She swallowed slowly. Soon she would have the relief she had prayed for. No more pain.

"From dust we are and to dust we do return. May God remember this poor suffering soul in the ressurection where mankind will at last have peace in a world free of sickness and death."Gussie hugged Alfie close as they left Cassie's grave. The heavy down pour of rain and dark sky made the dismal scene even worse. People hurried toward their cars. Alfie stopped in front of Jay and the children. They hugged each other and cried, not noticing the heavy rain. Cassie's parents soon joined the small bereaved group. Lou tugged at Gussie's arm. "Come on, honey. You'll catch your death of a cold. Remember our son."

Alfie looked at Lou and then at Gussie. "Oh, Gussie, how stupid to let you stand in this rain." She took Gussie's free hand and the three ran for her car. A man with a beard and hat pulled over his eyes watched from a small car parked near the grave site. He wiped the tears from his eyes. He adjusted the leather strap on his leg. Guy had loved Cassie. She had been a wonderful friend. What had happened to her? She had always looked like the picture of health. He knew he must finish what he had come to do in the next few days. The sweet feeling of having revenge had taken on a dull glow. Maybe it was the funeral. Maybe it was the fact this life would never be as it had been before. He knew that he still loved Alfie. But how much? After all, she had married Jim. And wasn't Jim responsible for this whole mess? He would miss Maria and Jose. He would always keep in touch with them, but their relationship would never be the same. And Trina was taking the changes pretty hard. And things had already started to change.

If he could just talk to Alfie for a few minutes. But it would be too dangerous. He had given Jerry his word that he would remain out of sight until he was given the okay.

Alfie could hardly see the road. The windshield wipers didn't seem to help. Lou broke the silence. "A good, hot cup of coffee and a change of clothes will do wonders. Too bad Jim couldn't make it. Never knew of him to be sick before." Gussie nudged Lou with her leg. Alfie sighed. "He isn't sick. He hates funerals. Something to do with his childhood. I would have told you before the day was over. Jim has changed so much lately, I don't even know him. I guess I never did." Alfie pulled the car into the garage. Several cars were already parked in front of the house. Alfie hoped that the young girl she hired had everything ready. Jay and the girls were sitting in the living room with Cassie's parents, steaming cups of coffee in front of them. Jesse and his girlfriend were taking off their coats. Sarge was sitting in the big overstuffed chair talking to Cassie's parents. Their voices were low.

Alfie opened the bedroom door. The shades were still pulled. Jim must still be sleeping. She slipped off her shoes and pulled the dress over her head. She was soaked to the skin. She pulled her pantyhose off and gathered the wet clothes in her arms. She gasped as Jim's hands gently rubbed her cheeks He kissed her neck and pressed her body hard against his.Alfie felt a knot form in her stomache, she was going to be sick. She turned and pushed Jim away. Sex was the last thing she wanted, she had just watched her dearest friend being buried. She said, "Jim, please, not now." Jim smiled as his arms went around her waist, pulling her close once again as his lips silenced her. Alfie pushed at his chest as she struggled to free herself, he was hurting her. She bit his lip, his mouth pressed down on hers ever harder. She could taste his blood as he lifted her and carried her to the bed. He dropped her, then lowered his body on top of hers. He said, "If you ever bite me again, I'll kill you." Alfie looked into the cold unfeeling eyes of the stranger that lay above her and knew indeed, he would kill her. Her hand covered her bruised mouth to stifle a scream as Jim violated her body, taking liberties that Alfie had never even dreamed of. Alfie sobbed as she pleaded for him to stop. He rolled off, smug and satisfied. He said, "Now go to your friends, I'm sure they're wondering what happened to you." He laughed as he sat on the side of the bed and reached for his pipe. The shower seemed to sooth Alfie's bruised body. She would wait for everyone to leave before she told Jim she wanted a divorce. How could she have been so blind. Fresh tears spilled down her face. She dressed quickly as she avoided looking at Jim.

He tapped his pipe on the edge of the oversize ashtray and began refilling it with fresh tobacco. Jim stood up and reached for his clothes. He said, "I guess I should make an appearance. What do you think?" Alfie couldn't believe that he was acting as if nothing had happened. Her body burnt with the hatred she felt for him. She said nothing as she walked out of the bedroom door, closing it softly behind her. She looked at her watch. She couldn't believe that only 35 minutes had passed. Jim looked out the window. The rain was coming down in sheets. He heard the bedroom door close. The ocean waves were huge and angry. They were that way the day Guy had drowned. He couldn't forget the surprised, helpless look he had seen in Guy's eyes as he pried Guy's hands from his arm. Jim shook his head. How could he be so ruthless?

And the dreams he had started to have every night. Nightmares, not dreams. The little men in their funny suits, talking in a language he couldn't understand. Pulling him into the ocean and holding him under the water, bringing him up just before he drowned. They did this over and over until his lungs were on fire, ready to burst. His eyes felt like pepper had been poured into them from the salt water. And every time they would bring him up, a giant standing in the middle of the ocean with snow-white hair and a white beard, draped in a blood-red robe, with a scepter in his right hand and a glow around him as bright as the sun, would point the scepter down at him and the little men would push him back under the water. He would feel the seaweed winding around his chest, tighter and tighter. A pink bubble hovered over the giant's head and in it he could see the outline of two figures with their faces pressed against the bubble, waiting for his death. His heart and lungs seemed to burst at the same time and blood spurted from his mouth, ears and nose. His eyeballs popped from their sockets. Defecation ran down his legs. The little men pulled the body further into the ocean and tied a rope around his ankle. The rope was attached to an anchor that pulled his body to the ocean floor where it was to remain throughout Eternity with the fish nibbling on his flesh. He shivered. He would take the sleeping pills that slimy, quack doctor had prescribed for him. So what? he thought. Sleeping pills were sleeping pills. He pulled on his shirt and tucked it into his slacks.

Alfie looked up. Jim was embracing Cassie's children. She hadn't seen him come in. Jim walked toward the bar with Jesse and Lou at his side. She heard him say, "Must have been a touch of stomach flu. I feel fine now." Alfie walked over to Kat, the girl hired to help for the day. Mounds of food still lined the buffet table in the dining room. She smiled at Kat. "Did anyone eat? It certainly doesn't look like it." "Not much," Kat answered as she started clearing the table. "I'll put out the cheesecake. Would you like me to make a fresh pot of coffee?" "Yes, please do, and whatever food is left, Jay can take home. And Kat, take some of it home for yourself and Daniel." Alfie walked over to the picture window. Outside, the rain drops were the size of half-dollars. She loved the sound they made as they hit the glass. The dismal weather matched her mood. She wanted to be alone. She wanted to sit and watch the rain in her soft, overstuffed chair. She wanted to cry, letting all the pain and agony she felt be washed from her body. She wanted to be ten years old again and feel the happiness she had felt then as she trailed behind Guy all over the Island, asking a million questions as he answered her with the patience a fifteen year old boy shouldn't have. She felt a hand on her arm. She looked into the gentle loving eyes of Uncle Frank. He wiped the tears from her cheeks with a soft tissue. She laid her head on his shoulder, smelling the pipe tobacco in the wool tweed of his sports coat.

Why couldn't she turn the clock back? Why?

chapter twenty nine

WITH WHAT MEASURE YOU MEET IT SHALL BE MEASURED TO YOU AGAIN

HUGE PINE TREES HID the house from the road. The house must be 200 years old, Jerry thought. Something from a child's fairy tale about knights and dragons. He felt as if a drawbridge should come down to help him enter this greystone castle. Instead, he walked up to the tall doors and lifted the heavy brass knocker, letting it fall against the thick wood. The door was opened by one of the fattest men that Jerry had ever seen. Small, beady eyes set in a giant balloon face with double chin after double chin. His head balanced itself on a body that filled the entire space of the door. There was no seeing around the sides of him. Jerry suppressed a grin by thinking about being crushed by one of the giant legs. What a horrible death that would be. Jerry clutched his attach case tighter as if this fat slob before him might grab it. "Yeah, what do you want?" the small slit in the balloon face opened. "Mr. Borenelli ain't in." "Wow," Jerry thought. "What finesse." The slob's voice matched his body at least, Jerry smiled. "I have an appointment with Mr. Borenelli. He's expecting me. My name is Jerry Easterman." The slob turned with a grace that belonged only to a ballerina. "Unbelievable," Jerry thought. The slob said, "your attache case. Dis way, follow me." Jerry followed down a dark, long, narrow hallway. The slob opened his attache case and examined the contents as they walked.

They stopped in front of double doors. The slob knocked and handed the attache case back to Jerry. The door was opened by a man in his late thirties dressed in a dark blue pin striped suit and a baby blue shirt which was opened at the neck. A heavy gold rope chain with a large eagle lay on his hairy chest. His black patent shoes sparkled like glass. His manicured hands seemed to be weighted down by his gold rings. His after shave was definitely, Lagerfled. His deeply tanned face was handsome. He had a small cleft in his chin, piercing, deep-gray eyes and white, even teeth. He held out his hand. Jerry shook it. "Mr. Easterman, I'm Jacob Borenelli. Come in." The door closed, leaving the slob on the other side. Jerry looked around. The room was tastefully decorated in brown leather and dark oak. Deep-wine drapes covered the windows. "Please call me Jacob and I'll call you Jerry." He motioned toward an oversized leather chair. "Please sit down." Jerry sank into the chair. Jacob sat opposite him. A dark, round oak table held a silver tray with hot coffee and a decanter of brandy. A maid entered through a side door. She sat a small tray of finger sandwiches on the table and poured the coffee and brandy. She opened two silver boxes. One held cigarettes, the other cigars. She looked at Mr. Borenelli. "Will there be anything else?" Jacob didn't bother turning his head, but dismissed her with a wave of his hand. He lifted the brandy to his lips, "Cordon Bleu. Excellent taste." Jerry tasted the brandy, holding it in his mouth a few seconds before swallowing. Cordon Bleu had always been a little heavy for his taste. But he said, "Yes, excellent brandy." Jacob sat the brandy snifter down and reached for a cigar.

"Tell me, Jerry, why Dominic Paveretti should be of interest to you." Jacob drew deeply on his cigar. "Are you a friend of his? Do you know where he is? Why did you come to me?" Jerry reached into his briefcase, pulled out a folder and handed it to Jacob. Jacob opened the folder. "Antonio and Ranelli, Private Investigators." A description and a small snapshot of Dominic Paveretti was attached to the left hand side of the folder. Jacob contained his burning hate and anger as he looked at Dominic's photo. His face showed no emotion. He read the report, never once looking up. He knew Antonio and Ranelli were two of the best private investigators in New York. They were also the most expensive. He also knew almost everything that was in the report. After all, it had been the governor, his father, that Dominic had killed. His expression remained the same as he read that Dominic Paveretti was now Jim Newman and that he lived on Pink Shell Island. But his heart was pounding wildly. He thought of his boys, Canto and Lonnie. They had been making a fool of him. They had probably known all along where Dominic was. Dominic had been paying them off. That was it. He hoped it had been worth it, because he had a special job for them to do. The governor was your father, wasn't he?" Jacob closed the folder. He took a long drink of brandy. He looked up at Jerry. "So, what has this got to do with me? You'll have to leave, Mr. Easterman. I have some important business to take care of. I'm sorry, but I don't know how I can help you. You've come to the wrong person. Jacob stood up. "Now, if you will excuse me." Jerry noticed that they were no longer on a first-name basis. "Wait, Mr. Borenelli, please. All I want is to have Jim Newman off of Pink Shell Island and to make sure that he stays off. He ruined my brother's life. I don't particularly want the man's blood on my hand, but I will do what I have to do. He did kill your father. I would imagine that you've wanted him for a long time." Jacob's back remained to Jerry. "Good day, Mr. Easterman." Jacob pulled on a cord hanging at the corner of the room, then walked out of the side door. Jerry turned toward the double doors as the fat slob entered. "Dis way, follow me." Jerry reached for his attache, case, realizing that Jacob had kept the folder. He smiled and started the rented Volkswagen.

Guy would be waiting to hear the good news.

chapter thirty

THE COUNT DOWN

JUAN LOPEZ HAD ALWAYS wished Trina would talk to him, confide in him. It had been hard raising a daughter alone, being both father and mother to her. Maybe he should have remarried after Trina's mother died. It was a little late to think about that now. He wanted to blame everything on the gringo. He had warned Trina not to get involved with Anthony. Now her heart was breaking. All she wanted to do was stay in her room. He would hear her in the bathroom throwing up and crying. She was making herself sick. He would ask Maria to come and talk to her. Maybe that wasn't such a good idea. Every time someone mentioned Guy's name in front of Maria, she would start crying, too. The gringo seemed to have touched the lives of everyone in the village of Baha Nye. Juan Lopez sighed heavily. He too would miss the boy when he left the village. Trina dried her eyes. The medicine had not made her abort the baby. What was she going to do? Where could she go? She would try the "slippery elm." It worked for her girlfriend, Carla. Maybe, just maybe, nothing was working because she really wanted to have the baby. But she could never tell Guy that she was pregnant.

chapter thirty one

THE HEART BREAK

THE HEAVY RAIN CONTINUED as Guy drove slowly to the small inn on the north side of the pier. He felt tired. He loved to sleep when it rained like this. The small room felt damp. He opened the drapes. Just removing his artificial leg was an effort. His body began to relax as he lay across the bed and watched the rain beating against the window. As thoughts of the past tried to seep into his mind, he pushed them away. The shrill ring of the phone jarred him. Jerry's voice was filled with concern. he said, "Why are you there? I thought we agreed to let New York handle it." There was a pause. Guy answered, "And, in the meantime, I watch him have free rein over my house, my business and my wife?" Jerry knew he had to pick his words carefully. He could hear the tension in Guy's voice. Before he could answer, Guy said, "Jerry, did you know that Cassie died? I should have been at the funeral with everybody else. Not sitting in a car on the side of the road watching them lower her body into the grave." "Stop it, Guy. You're talking like a fool. What happens when you're behind bars for life? Do you think anyone cares about your reasons for getting rid of him? Kill Jim, then someone else will have your house, your business and your wife. I'm catching the next flight out. Don't even move until I get there." The receiver clicked in Guy's ear. Guy strapped on his leg. The drive to the pier was a short one. The rain had slacked off, but the black clouds covering the sky gave promise of more, very soon.

The twenty steps to the top of the pier seemed like a hundred and twenty. He sat on one of the small benches. The old pelican perched on the rail close by. Guy jumped as someone sat down next to him. The rain had started to come down harder. He turned and squinted, trying to see who had intruded upon his privacy. Old Sarge said, "I'm glad you're alive. Why the mystery game? Don't you want Alfie to know or does this have something to do with Jim?" Guy was silent. "Let's get out of the rain. I have a bottle of brandy at my house and I think we could use it." Sarge took Guy's arm and guided him along the pier to the steps. They descended slowly. Guy was glad the rain hid the tears that blinded his eyes. Once inside the car, Guy said, "How did you know?" "Oh," Sarge hesitated before answering, rubbing the soft white beard on his chin. "'The Old Man in the Sea' told me. But I'll be danged if I know why he took so long to do it. Usually he tells me things right away. `Specially when it has to do with our own. I mean, the people on the Island." Sarge sucked on his unlit pipe. He glanced at Guy out of the corner of his eye. "Sure," Guy said. "And did he tell you I lost my leg to a shark after Jim tried to kill me? Did he tell you that I had amnesia for over a year?" Guy pulled up in front of Sarge's cottage. He turned and looked at Sarge. "Well, did he?" Sarge looked into Guy's piercing blue eyes and said, "No, he didn't." Sarge opened the car door and stepped out. The rain seemed to drench his clothes instantly. He looked back at Guy. "Come on. Hurry." The cottage was spotless. Small replicas of famous fishing boats sat all around. Guy walked over to the fireplace. Sarge handed him a robe. "Here, put this on. I'll lay your clothes over the back of the kitchen chair to dry out."

Guy pushed the reclining chair back, bringing his legs up. He lifted the brandy to his lips. His whole body felt relaxed. He opened his eyes and found himself staring into the eyes of the "Old Man in the Sea." The giant, with his body draped in white, had his feet planted firmly on the ocean floor. He held a scepter in his right hand and his snow-white hair and beard emitted a strange light that seemed to radiate from the picture and bathe the entire room in a soft glow. Guy guessed that the picture must be hundreds of years old. And he couldn't fail to notice that the man in the picture bore a striking resemblance to Old Sarge. He took another drink of brandy and studied the picture more closely. There was a pink bubble suspended in mid-air on the right of the Old Man's head. Two figures pressed against the sides of the bubble. Suddenly he knew that he was in the pink bubble. He was one of the figures trying to see out. The bubble seemed to become clearer. He saw little men in funny suits of all different colors. They were tying a rope to one ankle of a man. A dead man. The figure next to him sucked in a breath and held it as if shocked by the scene below. The face of the dead man floated up to them. It was Jim Newman. The figure next to him grabbed him and breathed out slowly. He squeezed the soft arm. He turned to the figure. It was Alfie. He gathered her in his arms. Oh, God, she felt good. She was crying as she whispered in his ear, "I love you. Why did you think I would care about your leg. I never want to lose you again. I've loved you all of my life." Nothing else mattered. Time stood still. He knew she was all he had ever wanted as he told her, "I'll always be with you. I've loved you always, too." The figure in his arms began to fade. The bubble vanished and before he had time to wonder what was happening, he was back in the chair and Sarge was saying, "Your Uncle was one of the best fishermen alive. I sure do miss him. We were good friends, you know."

Guy said, "Yes, I know. I miss him, too." "He would tell you the same thing I have. Don't take this matter into your own hands. By law, Alfie and Jim were never married. If this had happened anywhere else, she would have had to wait seven years because there was no body recovered. Alfie married him because she was lonely, not because she loved him. She also figured that he had been your good friend and that made it easier to accept. Women think that way. How would she know that he had been a hired killer?" Guy looked at him. "How did you know that?" Sarge looked old and tired as he sat in his easy chair. His shoulders slumped, "I haven't known it for long or I wouldn't have let Alfie get herself in this mess." There was a knock at the front door. Guy jumped. Sarge pushed his body out of the chair. He motioned for Guy to stay where he was. Sarge cracked the door. Guy heard voices. He pushed the recliner into a sitting position and stood up, reaching for his cane. He glanced up at the picture. There was no pink bubble and there were no little men in the picture. He turned, almost colliding with a small man in a tweed sports coat. It was Uncle Frank. They embraced each other. Uncle Frank took his handkerchief from his hip pocket and blew his nose. he wiped tears from his eyes with the back of his hand. Oh, it was good to be home. Guy embraced the old man again. Uncle Frank wanted to know everything.

chapter thirty two

THE TENSE MOMENTS

JIM WAS GLAD TO see everyone finally leave. He hated funerals and people crying. In fact, he was fed up with everything in general. The Island irritated him the most. It was so confining. He would have him and Alfie off this Island soon, very soon He pulled on his raincoat and without bothering to tell Alfie that he was going out, he began walking toward the pier. He noticed a small black sedan parked across the street from his house. If he didn't know better, he would swear it was one of the mob.He laughed. Those dumb jerks couldn't find their own shadows. Anyway, his protection was paid for. Canto and Lonnie would never set him up. The rain almost blinded his vision. Someone was running and shouting behind him. He turned to see Lou running toward him,. Jim said "whats wrong?" But Lou was out of breath from running and Jim had to wait for him to answer.

"It's Gussie. She's in labor. We've got to get her to a hospital." Jim and Lou ran back to the house. Alfie was in the bedroom with Gussie. She was wiping the sweat from her forehead. Lou felt helpless as he said, "I was trying to call for help, but the phone lines are down." "Come on," Jim said, "let's get her into the car. We shouldn't take any chances. If I go for help, I may not be back in time." The windshield wipers were practically useless as the down pour made visibility zero. They were making poor time. Gussie's groans increased, though Lou was trying valiantly to comfort her. Alfie's knuckles were white as she clutched the dashboard, squinting to see things that Jim might miss. She screamed as the old white truck seemed to appear from nowhere. Jim turned the wheel and slowly mashed the brakes, afraid too much pressure on them would turn the car over. The car skidded sideways and came to a halt on the opposite side of the road. No one was hurt. "Thank God," Alfie whispered. Jim got out of the car, everything looked okay on the outside. Alfie reached back and patted Gussie's knee, "Don't worry, honey, we'll be there any second now."

Gussie managed a weak smile as she said, in a voice barely above a whisper, "I'm okay. It's probably just false labor. I know Guy will get me there." Jim was silent. His eyes strained to see the road. A muscle twitched at the corner of his mouth. Alfie knew that Gussie didn't realize what she had said. She hoped that Jim had not heard her, but she couldn't concern herself with that now. She must concentrate on her prayers that Jim would make it to the hospital safely.

Jim thought that no one else had heard Gussie use Guy's name. He felt that old pang of guilt. He had really liked Guy. Guy had been kind to him when few men ever had. If he hadn't been attracted to Alfie, things could have been much different. Jim had fancied that one of his brothers might have looked like Guy if he had lived. Christ, he thought. I must be getting soft. Two orderlies rushed out to the car with a wheelchair. The three sat in silence in the tiny hospital waiting room. The only sound was the rain as it hit the window. Alfie wanted to call Uncle Frank, but the phone lines were still down.

chapter thirty three

SURPRISES IN MEXICO

JUAN LOPEZ'S MOUTH HUNG open in surprise and disbelief as he heard Trina say, "Papa, Polo and I were married this afternoon. Please don't be angry. I love him, Papa." Juan hugged his daughter as she sobbed against his chest. Polo thought that his new bride was weeping with joy, but Trina and Juan knew the real reason. Maria was preparing the food for the wedding reception. She knew why Trina had married Polo. He was a good man, and would make a good father. Maria had known that Trina was pregnant long before Trina had known herself. There was no need to tell either Juan or Polo. A lot of babies came early. She also knew Trina had tried to get rid of the baby. The old woman, Enriquetta had told her. Maria had paid Enriquetta to give Trina the wrong medicine. After all, the baby Trina carried belonged to Guy. And she was going to be the godmother. Maria hummed as she continued cooking, placing the last tamale in the tall pot.

Guy had called the inn where he was staying and had left Sarge's number at the desk in case Jerry should call him. The rain continued to pour down. Sarge held the phone out to Guy. "It's Jerry. He just got in." "I'm glad to be on the ground. Rough flight. Are you okay?" "Yeah, I'm okay. How are you getting here? I know the cabs won't drive in this mess. Why don't I drive over and get you?" "No," Jerry said. "No way. I'll hang around here until there's a let-up then grab a cab. It can't rain forever. I imagine that there's a lot to talk about. I'll call before I leave unless you expect to stay where you are." "Yeah, I'll be here. No sense in driving back to the inn. Sarge and Uncle Frank want to see you. We'll be waiting here." As Guy hung up the phone, he heard Uncle Frank say, "I never liked Jim anyway. There was always something sneaky about him."

chapter thirty four

THE GROUND WORK

KYLE FINISHED MAKING LOVE to Cookie, he just couldn't see her any more..When he did he always feel so guilty? A man couldn't wait like a woman could. But was it worth Jill finding out about cookie? No, he was in love with Jill. When he made love to Cookie he thought of her. But Jill would remain a virgin until their wedding day. The very mention of them going "all the way" made Jill burst into tears. He wanted her so badly. He had to get relief somewhere, and decided that he might as well pay for it. And he knew Cookie would never say anything. But Kyle had made up his mind nothing was worth losing Jill Kyle looked at his watch. Jeeze, he was supposed to be on duty ten minutes ago. The rain was coming down in buckets. Kyle unlocked the patrol car. Oh, man, his radio. Someone was already trying to reach him. He switched the button of his radio on. "Officer Jeffries, where the samhill are you?"

Oh, no, it was the Sheriff. "I'm here, Sheriff. I had to use the restroom. Upset stomach, sir." "Listen, Jeffries. There's a black sedan that's been parked across the street from Alfie's for two days. Check it out and get back to me. I'll be at Sarge's house."

chapter thirty five

THE SEPARATION

JIM HAD TO HAVE a smoke. "I'll be back in a minute." He walked from the waiting room. Alfie patted Lou's arm. "It won't be long now, she's in the delivery room. Try to relax." She smiled. Was she telling Lou to relax, or herself? She thought of Jim and shivered. Other than the fact that he hadn't spoken to her there was no indication on his part that their marriage had fallen apart. Alfie had reached a decision. She would tell him today, after she saw that Gussie and the baby were alright. It had been a mistake from the beginning. She knew that he cared for her in his own strange way, but she had never really loved him. She had just needed someone. And he had been there at her weakest moment, when she felt the loss of Guy the most. She had needed a man to lean on and he had always been around with the right words to reassure her. How stupid she had been. She had never really known Jim and she didn't know him now. She had been weak and vulnerable and taken advantage of his willingness to be there. She could see it now. A nurse appeared in the doorway. "Mr. Phillips?" "Yes, I'm Phillips. Is my wife all right?" The nurse smiled. "Yes, and so is your eight-pound, fifteen ounce son. Congratulations." Lou shouted, "Hot dang! I've got me a boy. Did you hear that, Alfie. I got me a boy. Yahoo!" He hugged Alfie and danced around the floor. Alfie was laughing. She had never seen anyone so happy. The nurse tapped Lou's shoulder. "You can see the baby now and then we'll take you to your wife's room." "Wait, I want Alfie to go with me. Come on, Alfie." The nurse raised her stern voice. "Mr. Phillips, only one visitor at a time. Mrs. Phillips is very tired." She raised her hand. "I must insist." "You go on, Lou. I'll see what Jim's doing. I'll be back in half an hour." She kissed his cheek. "I'm so happy for both of you."

Jim was not in the gift shop. "Hmm," thought Alfie. Maybe he went into the cafeteria. The cafeteria was almost deserted. She walked back out the door. It was four p.m. and the sky looked black. The heavy rains continued. There was no other noise except the click of her heels on the shining tile floor of the hospital. She followed the green line that led to the entrance of the hospital. She pressed her face to the glass and decided that she would have to do better than that if she were going to see anything. She pushed against the door. The wind had picked up a little more force. There was an awning from the front door to the steps. Alfie was thankful for that. She strained her eyes searching for Jim. She spotted the old black sedan sitting across the street and realized that it was the same car she had noticed in front of her house. The sky was a blanket of gray. The rain had slackened to a drizzle. Alfie walked to the steps. The black sedan pulled slowly away from the curb, revealing an inert bulk lying in the road. Alfie strained to see what it was, thinking that maybe the people in the sedan had dumped their trash out. The nerve! Littering was one of Alfie's pet peeves.

She walked down the steps to have a closer look.

chapter thirty six

THE GROUND WORK CONTINUES

KYLE HAD FOUND THE sedan and had checked it out. The sedan had been rented. Punker and his dad, Albert Hailey, owned the only two car rentals on the Island, and Kyle was on his way now to talk to Punker. Punker sat looking at the empty lot. There wasn't one car left to rent. His dad would be happy about that. Kyle pulled into the empty lot. Punker walked toward the patrol car. That long, easy stride of his made Kyle feel real lazy. Punker never hurried. No need to he thought, unless, there was an emergency. And there never had been. Anyway, he remembered what his mom always told him. "Take it easy, son. When you're dead and gone all of this will still be here." A sweep of her hand waved across the Island and the ocean around it. She had been right too. His mom was dead, but life on Pink Shell Island was just as it had always been.

Punker leaned on the side door of the patrol car. His breath smelled of strong tobacco. Turning his head, he spit out the dark juice letting it join the water that rushed down the gutter. The rain had finally stopped, but the dark sky held a promise that it would pour down in sheets again soon. Punker grinned. The dark stains of the chewing tobacco covered his teeth. "What happened to you Saturday? Me and Christy thought you and Jill were going with us to the Lobster House. They had a good band. A new group called Porkie's Five Alive." Kyle was wondering what had attracted Christy to Punker. Christy was tall and thin with hair the color of burnished copper splashed with deep cherry highlights, and she was clearly devoted to Punker. She clung to his every word, as if he were the smartest man around. Punker did seem to be pretty smart, Kyle had to admit that. He was doing well financially and seemed to be making more money all the time. He wasn't handsome but looks weren't everything. He treated Christy as if she were a twenty carat diamond, women respected him for that. Kyle showed Jill a similar respect. He was more than anxiously awaiting the day when they would be married. Six more months and she would be his...all the way. Dang, he could hardly think about it without a hot feeling engulfing his body.

Punker spit again. The dark juice landed in the gutter. It started to rain again. "Come on, let's go inside," Punker said. Kyle turned off the engine in his patrol car and rolled up the window. Even though they ran, they were both soaked before they reached the small building. "Jeeze," Kyle said, peeling off his jacket. "Will this rain last forever?" Punker laughed. "Sure looks like it." Punker poured two cups of steaming coffee. "Here, this will warm you up. You never did tell me what happened to you on Saturday." Kyle sipped at the coffee. "I may never get any free time. Jesse's got me on this case. Must be a big one." "You know the black sedan you rented out a couple of days ago? Here's the license number. Who did you rent it to?" Punker took the paper with the license number on it. He walked over to his desk and sat down and ran his finger down a ledger. "Here it is." Punker frowned. "They're hoods, aren't they? I told Dad soon as they came in here not to rent them the car. There was trouble stamped all over them. Dad's not as perceptive as he used to be. As he gets older, he's more trusting of everyone.

"Now, wait a minute. I didn't say they were hoods. I don't know who they are or where they came from. If I did know something, I couldn't talk about it because all police business is strictly confidential." "On the other hand, if they had rented a car from you..." Kyle grinned. "What did they look like and where did they say they were from? I need all the information I can get." Punker handed Kyle the ledger. "We have to see a driver's license before we let anyone rent a car. Here's what his license said." "Hmm, interesting." Kyle scanned the information from the New York driver's license. Leonard San Angelo. "Sounds like an Italian name. What did they look like?" Punker popped the top from a soft drink can. He looked at

Kyle. "Want one?" "No thanks. I haven't finished this coffee. Well, what did they look like?" "The one that gave me his driver's license was tall and thin. He had a mustache that looked as if it were sketched on with a pencil. The other one was shorter, with muscles like a weight lifter. Both of them had black hair and dark skin, and they were sharply dressed...suit, tie, the whole works. Not bad looking. They told me that they were here to buy property, though I hadn't asked for a reason. I thought it strange that they should volunteer something like that." Kyle took down the information on his note pad. He handed the ledger back to Punker. "How long were they keeping the car? Was there anything unusual about them...scars, rings, anything?" "Yeah, they looked like a couple of gangsters, the kind you see in the movies. They're paying for the car with a credit card. They thought they would need it a week, maybe less."

Punker took a long swig of his soft drink. "There's gonna be trouble, I can feel it. Who are they looking for?" "Why do you think there will be trouble? Punker, if you mention this to anybody, I'll be in deep shit. Jesse will think I've been telling everybody our secret police business, and I really haven't told you anything." Kyle got up and walked to the window. A loud roar of thunder ripped through the sky. It had been a long time since he'd seen it rain like this. Punker eyed a cockroach as it make a slow, steady trek across the floor. There weren't many of them around here. He stood up and pushed his chair back. His big shoe came down on the roach. He hated bugs of any kind. Punker walked over to the window and stood beside Kyle. "Have I ever done anything to get you in trouble? Are we best friends?" Kyle laughed. "Yeah, we sure are. I'm just a little nervous. I didn't mean that. I know you won't say anything." He patted Punker on the back. "I gotta go. Jesse's waiting for me at Sarge's house. We'll get together this Saturday, for sure, okay?"

Punker grinned. "Yeah, okay. Give me a call on Friday. And Kyle...be careful."

chapter thirty seven

THE DISCUSSION

THE FIVE MEN SAT around the fireplace staring into the roaring fire. The room was cozy and warm. Each man held a steaming cup of coffee laced with brandy and thick, sweet cream. Jesse could hardly believe what he had just heard. But he knew it was true. He'd never really cared for Jim. Now he knew why. He said, "I should be hearing from Kyle any minute." Jerry put his cup on the coffee table. "I think Jacob Borenelli sent those men to get rid of Jim. In fact, I'd be willing to bet on it. Why interfere? Let them do the job they were paid to do. You don't want scum like Jim living among decent, law-abiding people, do you?" "Listen Jerry, you know I want to see Jim get what's coming to him. All of you know that. I'll turn a blind eye long as no one else gets hurt. I think there's one thing you've all forgotten. I am The Law. I'm here to uphold law and order. I can't let two hoods run loose on my

Island. Not for long, anyhow." Guy held up his hand and said, "Hold it. Don't get excited Jesse. We know you feel the same way we do. And we know you're right. You have your job to do. I don't think those two men will hurt anybody besides Jim. Hired guns don't shoot anyone for free. I'm not trying to be funny...I honestly don't think they want any attention from the law."

Sarge said, "Guy's right. If they're professionals, they'll do the job and get out of here." "Yep," Frank said. "Give them a couple of days anyway." "Yeah, I guess you're right. I just don't like trouble." Jesse grinned. "But what are friends for?" Sarge held up his cup. "Let's toast to Jim's farewell."

Guy tapped his wooden leg. "Yes, a forever farewell toast."

chapter thirty eight

GAMES FOR ALL

JIM STOOD LOOKING THROUGH the front door of the hospital. The black sedan parked across the street was the same one he had seen at his house. There was no doubting it...they had found him. How? Canto and Lonnie. How else? The sensation he felt in the pit of his stomach was not fear. It was excitement. His senses became alert. He felt a surge of energy. His adrenaline level was at its peak. He smiled as he turned and walked toward the back of the hospital. He had to get to his car without being seen. He had a gun in the glove compartment. It wasn't the one he would have chosen, but it would have to do for now. He had parked on the street after letting Gussie off at the Emergency entrance. He disliked parking in lots; too many people would have a chance to dent it. The black sedan was parked in front of it now. Jim reached the back entrance of the hospital. He turned up the collar of his raincoat as he pushed the door open.

Calib was just parking the car when he spotted Jim. Why was he standing in the rain? Who was he looking for? Calib rolled the window down. "Jim, Jim, over here," Calib shouted, hoping Jim would hear him above the rain. Jim made a run for Calib's blue station wagon. Opening the door, he slid in. "What are you doing here?" Calib flushed with embarrassment as he pulled his raincoat tight around him. Jim smiled to himself. He could make Calib do anything he wanted him to. But hadn't he always known that?

Jim said, "I might ask you the same thing." "It's Lenny, " Calib said. "Last night he had a pain in his chest. We thought it was gas but it wouldn't go away. It finally got so bad I had to bring him here. I'm glad we did, though. The doctors said he had a mild heart attack. Can you imagine having a heart attack at age thirty-five? Lenny's the picture of health. The doctor said it was stress that brought it on. What stress? I don't think the doctors know what their talking about." Calib sighed. "Now, it's your turn. " Jim said, "Gussie's having the baby. She needs some papers that were left at home. I was going to get them for her but the car won't start. "Guess I'll call a cab. Tell Lenny I hope he gets better. Maybe I'll stop in to see him when I get back." "You won't be able to get a cab in this weather. I'll take you." Calib started the car. Jim placed his big hand on Calib's thigh and squeezed. "I wouldn't want you to go out of your way."

Calib's breath caught in his throat. Was Jim making a pass at him or was he dreaming?

Alfie pulled her raincoat tightly around her as she ran across the street. A plastic trash bag. Someone had probably used it to cover his head. What a place to dispose of it. She picked the bag up. She would throw it in the trash can. Alfie turned as the black sedan pulled next to her. "Can we give you a lift?" Canto flashed his big smile. His good looks always charmed the ladies. Alfie started to walk around the car. Lonnie grabbed her, taking the trash bag from her hands. He slid it over her head. She tried to scream as the plastic stuck to her face. She was thrown onto the back seat. Canto pressed the accelerator. The car skidded. Canto fought to get it under control. "Jeeze," Lonnie said. "Dat was a close one. Dat trash truck missed us by a silk thread. Whatcha trying to do, get us killed?" Canto laughed. "Stop yapping. I'm da expert driver. It ain't me, stupid." Lonnie poked a hole through the trash bag big enough for Alfie's nose. "Can ya breathe?" Alfie shook her head yes. She told her body to relax. Don't panic. What was going on? Who were these men? Now, how did that husband of yours get such a looker as you? She's a looker, Canto. What a pair of legs." Lonnie lifted Alfie's dress. His hand ran up her thigh. He ran his finger under the edge of her French-cut panties. He pulled them down and spread her legs. Alfie couldn't scream. And her hands had been secured behind her with a rope. Alfie pulled her leg back and kicked Lonnie in the head with all the force she had. Lonnie's head hit the car window. He saw stars. Canto screeched the car to a stop, pulling to the curb. He jumped from the car and swung the back door open. Lonnie tumbled from the car, holding his head in his hands. He groaned. Canto saw what Lonnie had been up to. He turned to Lonnie and his foot connected with Lonnie's stomach. Lonnie doubled over with pain. Canto caught him on the chin, straightening Lonnie back up, sending his body down on the sidewalk. Lonnie lay in a heap. Canto slipped Alfie's panties back on. "Don't worry, lady. Dat creep won't try anything like dat again." Alfie was crying as Canto sat her up. He tied her feet together. "Don't try notin funny. I'm gonna put the creep in the front seat with me. All we want is your husband. Okay?"

chapter thirty nine

THE SEARCH

JESSE STOOD UP AND stretched. "I'm going with Kyle. I want to tail those two men for a couple hours." Uncle Frank took a sip of his brandy-laced coffee. "They'll spot you in a second. Might as well go through the street shooting a gun as to go in that police car." "I'm not taking the patrol car. We're going in Kyle's Camaro. Right, Kyle?" Jesse patted Kyle on the shoulder. "Sure," Kyle said. Guy walked toward the door. He reached for his raincoat. "I'm going with you. I'll go nuts just sitting around." "Me, too," Jerry said. Jesse started to protest. He shrugged his shoulders. "Why not? Have you got a gun...just in case?"

chapter forty

BACK IN MEXICO

TRINA LOOKED TIRED. POLO tried so hard to please her. He waited on her dotingly. All of her friends were envious of the special treatment she received. She thought constantly of Guy and the baby that grew inside her. Guy's baby. Maria whispered to her on her wedding day, "Wait one month then tell him you are pregnant. A lot of babies come at seven months." Trina had not been shocked. Maria was a wise woman. Everyone knew that. She would do as Maria said. She knew Maria would tell no one else. If she could just stop the terrible ache in her chest. Would she ever stop loving Guy? Maria lit the candle then knelt at the altar. She prayed for everyone, especially Guy and his unborn child. Maria knew he would return. If not to stay, then to visit and to collect his belongings. She thanked God for the short time that Guy had been her son. That's what she had needed. A baby. How ridiculous for an old woman to feel like that. The tears spilled from Maria's tired old eyes. She had waited too long. Jose had a feeling that Guy needed help, but the rain had not let up for days. Should he chance taking a boat out in this weather? He would talk to Juan.

chapter forty one

THE GAME CONTINUES

CALIB PULLED UP IN the driveway. "Might as well come in. It might take a few minutes to find things." Calib was grateful for that. He had to use the toilet and relieve himself. Calib had a feeling of pride as he entered the house. It was beautiful, thanks to him and Lenny. "Make yourself at home," Jim winked. Calib headed for the toilet in the hallway. Calib heaved a sigh of relief as he started to flush the yellow liquid down the small hole of the toilet bowl.. He felt someone grab him from behind. The searing pain in his head was excruciating. Jim's fist brought spatters of blood from Calib's head and face that hit the floor and walls of the small bathroom. The names that were hurled at Calib were so vulgar that it made Calib wince. Calib had never been treated like that. Jim laughed as he pushed Calib to the floor and said "Clean up this mess, now!". Calib's tears were hot as they slid down his face. He cleaned the floor and wall of the small bathroom. And all of this time he thought Jim liked him.. He was sure that Jim must be upset about something, yes that must be it, he would do anything to please Jim, anything.

It had been a long time since Jim had stuck it to a fag,. He used to make a game of it in New York. If one bothered him too much, Jim would go along with it, then when the fag was on his knees . Jim would laugh as he blew his brains out. He loved to see the expression on their faces and the fear in their eyes when he put the gun to their heads. He couldn't do that to Calib, not right now. But soon, very soon. Calib slid behind the wheel.

"Wait," Jim said. "Don't you have a boat?" "Yes, why?" "Because I want to use it." Calib smiled. "You can use anything I have. Anytime." "Good," Jim said. "Take me to it." "What," Calib said. "You can't take the boat out in this weather. You'll drown." "We're taking the boat out. Maybe we'll both drown." Jim took his .357 magnum out and checked to make sure it was loaded. Calib's heart fluttered. He was terrified of guns. Christ, he thought. Jim's crazy. And just when he had fallen in love with him. Calib sighed as he turned the car around and headed for the boat dock.

chapter forty two

AT THE HOSPITAL

LENNY WATCHED THE HEART monitor. Where was Calib? Maybe he couldn't make it in this weather. They had almost wrecked last night on their way to the hospital. Lou walked by Lenny's door. Lenny stared. Why that was Lou, Alfie's brother-in-law. Did Lenny dare yell? "Lou, Lou?" He doubted that Lou would hear him. Lou stopped. Who was calling him? Lenny tried again. This time a little louder. "Lou, Lou?" Lou turned around and walked back to the door he had just passed.

"Well, I'll be darned. If it ain't Lenny. What happened to you?" Lenny dabbed at the fresh tears that had welled up in his eyes. Every time he thought about his situation, he felt sorry for himself. Lenny regained his composure. "The doctors said I've had a mild heart attack. Can you believe it?" "I'm sure sorry to hear that, Lenny. But you're young and strong.

You'll be okay. Just take it easy." "Thank you, Lou. But why are you here? Nothing's wrong with Gussie or Alfie, is there?"

"Nope. Nothing's wrong." Lou's face lit up like a candle. "But you can congratulate me. I just had a baby boy. Howard Thornton Phillips, III, after my daddy." "Oh, Lou. I'm so happy for you." Lenny blew his nose. He loved babies. Lou asked, "You haven't seen Jim or Alfie, have you? "I haven't seen anybody. I've been waiting for Calib all day. No one answered at the house. I just hope he's okay."

Lou tried Jesse's office. No answer. Alfie and Jim were gone. Calib couldn't be reached and no one was at Jesse's. He would try Frank's again. Maybe this time he could get through. Kathy answered the phone on the third ring. Kathy was excited. Why hadn't Lou called them earlier. Was Gussie all right? She gave him Sarge's phone number. Sarge answered. He handed the phone to Frank. Frank let out a yell. He said, "Let me speak to Alfie. Hot dog! A baby boy." And Gussie was fine.

Lou said, "Something funny is going on. Alfie and Jim are gone. I know Alfie would have told us if she were leaving. She hasn't even seen the baby. She went to find Jim and never came back. Their car is still parked out front. I'm kinda worried." "Maybe they're in the cafeteria or the bathroom?" "Nope," Lou said. "I've looked through every inch of this hospital." Frank hesitated. "Lou, there's a lot we have to tell you. Sarge and I are on our way. We'll try to find Jesse. Just stay where you are." The phone clicked in Lou's ear. "Now what?" Lou walked toward the nursery. Gussie was asleep. Lou got the nurse's attention. She rolled Howard over to the window. He was really something. This kid would never want for anything. Well, lookie there! Howard's mouth turned up at the corner. By golly, the kid was already smiling at his old dad!

chapter forty three

ABSOLUTE TERROR

CANTO PULLED UP ON the side of Alfie's house. Lonnie moaned in the front seat. Alfie's wrists and ankles hurt from the rope burns. Oh, dear God, would this nightmare ever end? And when it did, how would it end? Why did they want Jim? What had he done? So many questions and no answers. Canto shoved Lonnie. He tumbled from the seat. Lonnie stood up and leaned against the car. He looked at Canto and spit the dried blood from his mouth onto Canto's shoe. Canto grabbed him by the front of his shirt and pulled him up close. "How about me putting in a call to Borenelli. Would you like dat, stupid? We're not here to hurt anybody but Newman. You're a lunatic Lonnie. Shape up, man. If you need a broad so bad, we'll find you one after all dis is over." Canto slipped the bag off of Alfie's head and untied her feet. Her feet tingled as she stood up. "Just keep ya mouth shut and do whatcha told and you won't get hurt." Canto pushed Alfie ahead of them. Once they were inside, he untied her hands. He threw the gun to Lonnie. "Here. Keep her in sight. If she runs, you can shoot her. Just don't kill her."

Lonnie looked at Alfie. Blood was caked on the side of his mouth. Alfie wanted to throw up but she was afraid to even move. Lonnie sneered at her. "Run for it, you stupid broad." Canto came back into the living room. "The bathroom's down the hall. Go clean up. Give me da gun." Lonnie handed Canto the gun and walked down the hallway. "I have to go, too." Alfie's voice was almost a whisper. "Yeah, well it's being used." Canto shifted in his seat. "There's one in my bedroom." Alfie thought of the gun in the nightstand. If she could just get her hands on it.

"Get up. Walk in front of me and don't try nutin funny." Canto gave her a shove. "What do you want with my husband?" "None of your business, little lady. The less ya know, the better off ya are. All you have to do is cooperate and tell me where he's at." Alfie walked slowly toward her bedroom. She was glad she didn't have to look at his face. "I don't know where he is. I was looking for him when you and your friend shoved me into the car." "Yeah, well, we're gonna wait right here til he shows up.

Frank pulled the car into the parking lot. The rain had slowed to a drizzle. Lou was pacing up and down in the hospital lobby. He spotted Frank and Sarge making their way slowly down the hospital corridor. He was certain that their news was not good.

Calib tried to start the car again. There was only a clicking noise. "It's the starter. We were supposed to take it in tomorrow for repairs." Jim opened the car door. "Get out. It's less than a mile. We'll walk." The steady drizzle of rain soaked them to their skins. Calib shivered. He had never prayed in his life. Why did he feel this sudden urge now to do so?

Calib's boat was a 25-foot cabin cruiser. The name on the side of the boat read "Calib's Delight." The angry waves rocked the boat back and forth. Calib opened the small closet, pulling out dry clothes. "I always keep extra clothes stashed here. You never know when you'll need them." He handed a shirt and a pair of pants to Jim. "Is there anything to drink around here?" Jim buttoned his pants. The flannel shirt felt soft and warm against his body. A good slug of gin would warm his insides. Calib opened a cabinet, displaying a full stock of liquors. "I'll get it. You start this thing up." Jim poured the gin. Want one?" He held the paper cup out to Calib.

Calib drained the cup. A warm glow spread through his body. He thought of Lenny. Their life together had been serene. He knew that by now,

Lenny would be worried. Tears began to slide down Calib's face as he headed the boat out to sea with the waves tossing it back and forth.

The windshield wipers and the steady downpour of rain were the only sounds that could be heard in Kyle's car. The four men inside looked intently at the few cars that passed and at the ones parked along the curb. Guy's thoughts were far away. He thought of Maria and Jose. He thought of Trina and the visible pain on her face when he told her he could not get involved. And it had been true. And how could he have two futures - what a stupid thought. He had tried to tell her that from the very beginning. Why had he let her fall in love with him? When he had told her not to care about him that way, there had been no big scene, no crying, no accusations. In fact, she had simply turned and walked away. There was no questions from Jose or Maria as to why Trina was suddenly not around. His life had been slow and easy with them. But he was in love with Alfie. He always had been. And he was certain that she still loved him.

chapter forty four

NO CLUE

JESSE'S VOICE INTERRUPTED GUY'S thoughts. "Pull over next to that car Kyle. Looks like it's stalled, maybe the driver needs some help." Kyle pulled up next to Calib's station wagon. "There's no one in the car. Whoever was in it probably walked to a phone or to one of the houses around here for help.

Here's the registration. It's registered to Calib Dwardy. I thought it was Calib's wagon. I'm sure he'll take care of it. Let's go on up to the north end of the Island, Kyle." "What reason would Calib have to be out in this weather?" Kyle turned on the window defogger in his car. Guy was amused, thinking of Calib. "I guess nothing's changed much since I've been gone. So Calib and Lenny are still in the decorating business? Alfie always wanted them to decorate our house. I wonder if she ever got her wish." "Yeah," Kyle said. It wasn't too long ago. I was there this morning after the funeral. It's beautiful.

"Christ," Jerry said. "It's so hard to believe that Cassie would kill herself. Things seemed to be going so well for her. "I felt like doing the same thing about six months ago." Guy folded a piece of paper into a small square. "But I thank God that there were people around me who cared enough to stop me. I could easily have been where Cassie is." Jesse cleared his throat. He felt suddenly thankful for his life. He said, "Cassie had people who cared around her all the time. Her situation was a little different. She couldn't accept the fact that she was part Negro and she didn't think anyone else could accept it. Too bad she didn't take time to ask. I've never seen a man more crushed than Jay. If he didn't have those kids...Well, thank God he has them."

The car made its way slowly along the north shore. It would be dark in one more hour. Kyle spotted the sedan parked next to Alfie's house and pointed to it. Jesse said, "Let's back up about a block. We'll walk up to the house."

Lonnie dried his face. Sure got some nice stuff in this house, he thought. He looked in the mirror. He looked as if a professional boxer had worked him over. He walked back into the living room. So dat was the way Canto wanted to play. He wanted the broad all to himself. He was probably in the bedroom with her right now.

"And leave the door open. Be quick about it." Canto was feeling agitated. "But I can't go with the door open. Can I shut it halfway? You can see my legs," Alfie's eye pleaded. Jeez, women. Nothing was simple with them. They had to make everything difficult. "Yeah, okay. But only halfway." "Thank you," Alfie said. Is it okay if I get some Kleenex out of my nightstand?" "Next you'll wanna shower and change clothes." Canto ran his hand through his hair. "Go ahead. Hurry up." Alfie walked to the nightstand. She knew she would be dead if she made the wrong move, but she wasn't afraid. There was no other way. Lonnie looked into the first bedroom. His thoughts flashed back to his sordid childhood. His mom in her soiled housedress with her cigarette dangling from the side of her mouth. Six dirty little brothers and sisters. Never enough food or clothes. His mom had probably never even seen a place like dis. He couldn't help thinking dat his mom had deserved something like dis more than the broad in the bedroom did.

The giant waves were tossing Calib's boat around like a rubber raft as the salty water poured onto the deck. Calib shouted, "You're crazy. I'm turning back. We'll never make it to the mainland." Jim grinned. "I've already told you I can't go back. Either we make the mainland or we drown." Jim looked up. The grin disappeared from his face. Calib was sailing through the air, a shiny object in his hand. The cold metal burned like a fire as it penetrated Jim's shoulder. The pain was worse than getting shot. The heavy thud of the two bodies could not be heard above the loud roar of the ocean. The retort of the .357 magnum echoed silently throughout the dark.

Lonnie saw the gun in Alfie's hand before Canto did. Lonnie's scream startled Canto. He turned, catching Lonnie on the side of the head with his hand. Alfie started shooting. Her finger pulled the trigger again and again, until all the bullets were fired. Canto's gun had flown from his hand and slid across the hardwood floor to Alfie's feet. Alfie swooped it up and emptied the chamber. Canto's body lay across Lonnie's. Blood oozed from the bullet holes in his back. Alfie grabbed the billy club that was propped next to her bed that Jesse had given her for protection as she reloaded her automatic. Then she stood over the two bodies and emptied the automatic into them again. Only then did Alfie feel that it was safe to walk from the bedroom.

The four men began to run when they heard the gunfire. Guy's shoulder hit the door again and again until the door gave way. Alfie stood at the end of the hallway with the automatic clutched in her hand and her face drained of all color. Guy reached Alfie first. She looked into his eyes. The same eyes she had seen following her. The same eyes she had seen at Jonas' and at the edge of the house. She knew suddenly that they were the same eyes she had always loved. Alfie let out a sob as she fell into Guy's arms. She fit into them just right. She belonged in them. Guy held her tightly. His hands pushed her back just enough to taste her hungry lips and kiss the salty tears from her face. He would never leave her again. He was home. Alfie's body went limp in Guy's arms, the shock of everything had been too much. Guy lifted her and carried her to the sofa as Jesse went for the first aid kit in Kyle's car.

The power from Jim's .357 had blown Calib's body across the cabin of the boat, leaving a hole the size of a football through his middle. Jim pulled the knife slowly from his shoulder. "The stupid fag," Jim screamed as fresh blood poured down the front of his shirt. Jim tied the rope around his ankle. There, that should keep him from falling out of the boat. He couldn't see where the end of the rope was for all the water in the bottom of the boat. He knew it was tied to something. It had felt secure when he pulled on it. A huge wave hit the boat, turning it on its side. Jim grabbed the rope as his body started to slide. He was weak from the loss of blood. Oh No!, the rope wasn't holding. The anchor slid into the ocean. Jim's eyes widened in surprise as he tried frantically to untie the rope from his ankle. His efforts were in vain as the anchor pulled his body to the bottom of the ocean floor. His eyes remained open as his lungs burned like fire and his heart burst within his chest. Warm, red liquid ran from his nose and ears. Defecation ran down his legs.

The blue of the ocean looked like a cool sapphire under the warm sun, seeming so different from the raging nightmare of two nights ago. Alfie thought of her handsome new nephew, Howard. Gussie and Lou would take him home in a couple of days. They seemed so happy together. Alfie wondered if she would ever feel that way. She was so deep in thought that she didn't hear Guy come up behind her. She jumped when he touched her shoulder.

"I'm ready to go. Will you come with me to the dock?" He gathered her close in his arms, hating the thought of leaving her again even if it was only for a couple of days. "Yes, I'll come. Will you be back in time for Calib's services?" Alfie felt a lump form in her throat as she thought of Calib. Lenny had taken the news of Calib's death pretty hard. His doctor was concerned that Lenny might have another heart attack, but he had released him from the hospital last night in seemingly stable condition. Guy nuzzled his face against her neck. "I'll be back. The service is almost a week away. I don't want to go at all. You know that, honey. But I have to. Come with me." "Yes, I know you do" Alfie said,. I just hate to have you away from me again, but. you know I can't go. Not now." "Come on, before I get other ideas and miss my boat." He patted her on the behind. She signed heavily as she walked away. "Let me get my purse." She squinted as she walked into the cool, dark kitchen. Her eyes rested on Lou's tall frame. He was putting ice in a glass. "Hi, just getting some juice for Gussie." Alfie smiled. "Is the baby still asleep?" "Yeah. Seems like he wants to eat all the time. Gussie's worn out. He's a heavy little bugger. I'm glad she couldn't breast feed him. He'd have been on her breast all day." Lou laughed. Then noticing the pain in Alfie's eye's as he asked, is Guy leaving?"

"Yes. I'm going to the dock with Guy now. I'll see you in a little while. If I'm not back in time to cook dinner, just stick that turkey in the microwave. I made up some potato salad and a relish plate this morning. I might stop by Uncle Frank's for awhile." Lou said "don't worry about us, I haven't lived with a cook all my life."

Alfie carried her shoes in her hand as she walked along the shore. She stopped. A shiny object caught her eye. She bent down to pick it up. She caught her breath as her heart seemed to stop. Jim's diamond wedding band lay in the palm of her hand. What did it mean? She lay her shoes on the sand as she walked toward the ocean. She would throw the ring back. That's where it belonged. With Jim.

chapter forty five

RETURN TO MEXICO

MARIA CRIED AS SHE hugged Guy. "I have prayed to St. Anthony that you would soon come back. I missed you, my son. Will you stay? You won't believe what's happened." Guy hugged this kind gentle woman, feeling the love he would feel for a mother. She was the only mother he had ever known, the only one that had ever called him son. yes, he loved her. Jose hugged Guy as warmly as Maria had, but he knew that Guy had not come back to stay. Maria would have to realize that Guy had another life, but they could still see him and be a part of it. Guy put his arms around Jose's and Maria's shoulders. "Come on, let's sit down. We have a lot to talk about." Guy, Jose and Maria talked for hours.

"I am happy for you, Guy. Maria is happy for you, too." Jose nudged Maria's leg under the dining table. He had noticed the frown that had changed

Maria's face into that of an old woman. "Of course, I am happy for you." She squeezed Guy's hand and kissed the top of it. A tear fell on his skin and made him get up and gather the small kind woman in his arms. "Aren't you going to come and visit me? You know I want both of you to come often. I'm going to visit you, too. We don't have to stop seeing each other just because I wont' be living here. That is, unless you want it that way." Guy cupped Maria's face, lifting it so that his eyes met hers. "You know I never had a mother. Would it be all right if I called you Mother?" "Yes, I would like that very much, my son. I will come and see you often and you will always have a home here with us. Now, sit down. I made fresh tamales and fried beans." She smiled as she kissed his cheek. "I am just a sentimental old woman."

"Before I leave tomorrow, I would like to see Juan and Trina and, of course Carlos. How has Trina been?" "Trina got married to a young man she went to school with. They are very happy." Jose lit his pipe. Maybe it would be better if you did not see her this time. You do understand?" "Yes, of course I do. She deserves to be happy. She's a wonderful girl." Somehow the news of Trina's marriage upset Guy. That was ridiculous. Why should he be upset?

Alfie felt the sand shift under her feet. The water felt warm. She looked around. The beach was deserted. She stepped out of her shorts and halter top. She ran back, dropping them on the sand next to her shoes. She would swim for awhile. That always relieved the tension in her neck. The ring in the palm of her hand felt hot. She couldn't wait to drop it back into the ocean. Sarge walked along the sandy shore. The pink shells seemed more obvious today. Last night's dream had left him with an uneasy feeling, and seemed to make no sense at all. He had tried to save a woman from drowning, he couldn't see the woman's face because her long hair kept falling in front and hiding it. He hoped the dream meant nothing.

Gussie walked into the kitchen. "What are you trying to do, burn the house down?" She laughed as Lou looked up. He was trying to light the pilot on the gas oven. The microwave didn't seem to be doing the job so he had decided to stick the turkey into the oven. "You don't have to light the pilot. It stays lit. Have you tried the oven to see if it's working?" "No, I saw a movie once, it showed a man lighting a gas stove. Am I wrong?" Gussie laughed. "You're wrong. Here, let me show you how it's done." Gussie turned the oven on and slid the turkey in. "Why didn't you use the microwave? That's fast and easy." Lou cleared his throat. "Well, to tell the truth, I couldn't figure out what to do. Anyway, why are you out of bed, little lady? Is Howard alright?" "I'm out of bed because I feel great. And Howard's sleeping like a log. Where's Alfie?" "She went with Guy to see him off, and she said she might stop by Uncle Frank's on her way back. She looked kind of worried to me, but she has been through a lot the past few days.I know Gussie " I'll give Uncle Frank a call." "Dear God, I just hope she and Guy can forget the past and rebuild their lives from here on. Alfie deserves a good life. Why can't she have one?" Gussie took a sip of coffee.

Alfie dropped the ring. It vanished immediately. The water felt good on her naked flesh. She wouldn't allow herself to dwell on the past anymore. She would think only of Guy and their future. Nothing else mattered. She had been given a second chance with Guy and she wouldn't let anything get in her way. She had turned and was floating on her back when she heard someone shouting. She looked toward the shore. She hadn't realized how far she had drifted out. A man was waving his arms and shouting. He was pointing at something. It was then that she saw the shark. He was headed straight for her. Alfie dove deep. Maybe the shark would not follow her. She swam fast, her lungs burning from lack of air. How much longer could she hold her breath? Then from nowhere a school of porpoise surrounded her. She grabbed the fin on the back of one and it pulled her to the surface. It swam toward the shore with her as the others surrounded the shark. She let go when she felt the sand under her feet. Strong arms lifted her and she felt something soft being wrapped around her body. She welcomed the blackness that followed.

Alfie opened her eyes. Sarge said, "Good, you're awake. You gave me quite a scare, young lady. I'm too old for that much excitement. Here, drink this." Alfie drank the coffee and brandy. She stood up and walked over to the fireplace. She looked up at the picture of the "Old Man in the Sea." He looked a lot like Sarge. "I haven't seen or heard of a shark in these waters for years, " Alfie said. "I'm sorry I gave you such a scare. I found Jim's wedding band on the sand and I went into the water to throw it back. Sarge shook his head and said " "That was probably the "Old Man in the Sea's" way of letting you know that Jim was on the ocean floor and would stay there. I'm sure a lot of people wonder if he's dead or not. But we know," Sarge poured another shot of brandy into his coffee. "Your clothes are on the kitchen chair. Dress and I'll take you home." Alfie's face reddened as she remembered being naked. Sarge had put the soft flannel shirt on her. She slipped on her shorts and top.

Guy heard voices in the living room as he slipped his shirt off. The voices became louder. He had started toward the door of his bedroom when it burst open. Trina stood there. She looked wild. She had been drinking. "Ah, my pretty gringo. You come back. For what this time? Maybe you want to sleep with Trina again, eh? She threw back her head and laughed. Jose grabbed her by the arm. "Trina, don't do this. You will hate yourself tomorrow. You cannot blame Guy for being sick. It was not his fault." "I do not blame him for being sick. I blame him for making love to me when he felt no love for me. And now I carry his child." She twisted from Jose's grasp and ran. The surprised look on Jose's face matched that on Guy's. Maria was twisting the apron she wore.

Trina collided with Carlos at the front door. She fell into the coffee table. Guy grabbed her. She had lost so much weight. He held her close as she sobbed. Guy said, "Why didn't you tell me you were pregnant? Did you think I wouldn't care?" "I'm not pregnant anymore. I lost the baby weeks ago. I just wanted you to hurt the same way that I do. I wanted to tell you about the baby, but I knew you had your own life somewhere else. I loved you so much. I'm sorry. Can you forgive me?" "I just wish things could have been different. Can you forgive me?" Trina pushed herself away from Guy. She blew her nose. "I have to go. My husband is waiting for me. He is a good man. I will learn to love him.and forgive you? Maybe in time I can." Trina walked slowly out the door with Maria close behind.

Jose's eyes were big as he said," Carumba. What is happening? I knew nothing about this, believe me. Come, let us have a drink. I think we all need one." " I felt as if I had walked into a bull pen," Carlos said as he wiped his forehead with a handkerchief. "Make my drink a double." "Wait until Maria comes in and we will get to the bottom of this." Jose motioned for the men to sit down. Maria came into the kitchen. "I guess

I have a lot to explain, no?" Maria finished telling everything, except that Maria was still pregnant. "I guess a lot of it is my fault. I should have let Trina make her own decisions. Just because I am older, I feel I know what's best. Sometimes this is not true." Guy put his arm around Maria's shoulders. "Sometimes that is true with all of us. No one can make the right decisions all the time. We just do what we think is best. That's all we can do. I am the one to blame."

Jose took a long drink. The tequila burned as it went down. He followed it with salt and lime.. "I think Trina's life will take a turn for the best now. Her husband, Polo, is a good man. His gentleness and love will soon rub off on her." Carlos looked at Guy. "It is good to see you again. How long are you staying?" "I'm leaving tomorrow. My wife is waiting for me, too. So is my fishing business. But I want you to promise me that you and your family will come and visit us often. I owe you my life. You all are my family." Carlos smiled. "You are family to me, too. I will come and see you as often as I can and you must visit us often."

Maria set a plate of hot, deep-fried pork skins on the table beside a bowl of chili. The front door opened and a familiar voice called out, "Where is everyone?" It was Juan Lopez. He and Guy embraced. This would be a good night after all. "Tell me," Jose said. "How is your brother, Jerry?"

Trina leaned her head on Polo's shoulder. She felt her stomach. Soon they would be in Mexico City where they would begin a new life. It was a beautiful place to raise a child and tonight she would tell Polo she was pregnant. He would be so happy.

Alfie played with Ginny and Jay, Jr. "Okay, kids. Timeout. Let's get something to drink." Only one set of volleyball and she was out of breath. That was unusual. And this morning she had felt nauseous. It was probably all the excitement of the last few days. She couldn't wait for Guy to come home. He was due back anytime.

Lou had picked Gussie and Little Howard up and carried them both across the threshold of their home in Dallas. Boy, it felt good to be home.

Old Sarge sat on the pier with his fishing pole dangling in the water. He felt he must talk with the "Old Man in the Sea". He could feel that old uneasiness returning.

-- THE END --